# CASSINI'S VISION

**Brian Lavery**

This is a work of fiction. Similarities to real people, places, or events are entirely coincidental.

# CASSINI'S VISION

For Robyn.

Always the truth.
A Celi.
A Renna.

# Chapters

Are They returning, the Great Masters from beyond? Is this to be the Judgement, our final reckoning?

The Lady of those Rings, the rings around planet six, still waits and listens. The old creatures of the moon nearby no longer reply.

But someone did just pass by, chattering.

# Italy

"Take these lenses and search the heavens," said the dying man, "but publish and those earth-bound clerics will kill you."

Gian Cassini looked from the old fellow to the heavy glass.

"Young Cassini, all the forces in our world are desperate we should never reach the truth. I too beheld the skies, and I am since then imprisoned. But we are compelled to look. It's our only future. Sit near me."

Galileo opened his blinded eyes, and his hand trembled. But still he managed to find and to hold Cassini's forearm—a passing of the mantle.

But Gian did not yet have that vision.

# Cassini (b. 1625)

Gian's horse trotted along the narrow coastal track. Salt was in the boy's nostrils, and the sound of the small waves grew louder each time the track drew closer to the waterline. On the first Monday of each month, he would make this journey, to return on the third Thursday. On this first time, uncertain and anxious, he was escorted the entire trip by his Uncle's assistant.

Gian lived with his maternal Uncle Antonio Maria Crovese, and he had done since he was young. Antonio was Notary Public in Genoa, a man in touch with the business life of the region. The Uncle was happy to accept his role as tutor and guardian to this intelligent and likeable boy.

After three hours riding, when the morning was well advanced, the two riders could spy the township in the distance. Camogli was a bustling fishing village.

"I likely can meet you on your return day here in the town," said Leo. "I don't know the arrangements yet, but if we are to rendezvous here, we need to know how to find each other."

At the edge of town they stopped to stable the two horses. Leo knew Camogli. From here the long track to Gian's new school would be traversable only by foot.

They strolled past old cottages and around the pebbly beach by the fishing boats, arriving at a narrow tavern not far from the water, for lunch and cool drinks.

The old man tending the tavern recognised Leo at once. "You old renegade! Back in town, eh? And who do we have here?"

After the introductions and a secured promise to watch out for Crovese's young nephew should he turn up at the door in future, they ordered a fisherman's lunch, to be ready for the afternoon trek.

"We start there," said Leo, pointing, "the Church of San Rocco." Gian peered up to the old church, built worryingly high on the cliff to the south-east. From there the forested and mountainous peninsula looked it might lead them on forever.

The two walkers, packs now on their backs, trudged in the early afternoon up to San Rocco. Following a foot trail and many, many steps, they arrived at the church; it was locked. But from there a fine view across the bay to Camogli township and back towards Genoa was worth a break and a drink from their flasks.

From his pack, Leo took a new-looking pistol, more than two handspreads long. From a jar, he poured a quantity of black powder into the muzzle, and then a tiny ball. With a metal rod, he carefully rammed all that down into the barrel. He then tucked the weapon into his belt.

Gian was wide-eyed but silent. Leo didn't comment.

"Come on, Gian. That climb took us less than an hour." The walk, starting now through olive groves, became brisk but not strenuous. A small hut, lived-in, stood to the side of the olives and the trees were recently pruned. From there, the track narrowed and the forest closed in.

The path did not return to the coast. It stayed high in the mountains, winding upwards and downwards and up once more, with the trees tall, and the passage now wide enough only for one. Greenery and branches scraped them as they pushed through, and they could see little to the sides. The air was cooler here, but the walkers were warm.

After an hour, the trail started down again from the middle of the range. It was rocky underfoot, steep in places with many switchbacks to cope with the slopes.

Gian slipped again on the stones. "Now I know why I have these new boots."

When the stone buildings on the edge of the sea came into view below, Gian asked, "Why does it look so old?" The old Benedictine Abbey of San Fruttuoso. "Why is it so broken?"

"Because it *is* so old," replied Leo. "Some of those monastery structures were built five hundred years ago."

This Abbey had seen better times. "Little money is available to maintain it, and now no one can find enough use for all the buildings. We are a long away from town, remember."

For centuries, these coastal settlements had been vulnerable, too, said Leo, to the raiding corsair pirates, the Moors from the African Barbary Coast.

"See that more recent watchtower? That's used as defence from the pirates. The marauders come ashore looking for water and sometimes for slaves to take. Or sheep. Why do you imagine your Uncle sent me along with you? And you have so much more to learn here at the Abbey than Antonio could now teach you."

We'll see, thought Gian. Will they teach me more astrology here?

Carefully, Leo removed the pistol from his belt.

"As we enter, I'll need to hand this in for secure keeping."

"It's a Gavacciolo from Brescia," he added. "Gift to your Uncle for worthy services rendered. An experimental flintlock."

—

Leo had planned to return to Camogli village by foot track the same afternoon. For a price, however, the Abbey offered a sailboat return to Camogli. That would be a little later in the day when the wind was expected to pick up.

"Gian, that stone and mortar tower is intriguing me," said Leo. "We are allowed to go up. Come with me."

Living accommodation occupied the tower base. Small windows let in only a little light on the two as they laboured their way ever upward. A monk was on watch when they emerged onto the roof terrace.

"We use this lookout position," said the monk, "to see what ships may approach us. Often it's confusing because many vessels are our own. This and other towers along the coast also act as landmarks for ships to guide them in safety around the headlands and into their harbours.

"In past times, four or five men would be living at the tower all year, and the Abbey paid them. Now it's just us. If we see a suspicious ship that could be a pirate, we will light a fire on the roof here. The smoke will be seen down in the Abbey grounds and out at sea, and across the shoreline to that next tower you can see in the far distance. We blow a horn as well."

"I never realised there were more towers."

"Well, there are many, but most are smaller than this one. That other one you can see, it is not staffed a lot of the time, but we would light the fire in any case, in hope someone sees the alarm."

The terrace had defence walls with chutes, piombatoio, that could drop rocks or hot oil or water onto attackers. The lookout tower would be the last bastion in case of a major attack.

Gian said nothing. As always, though, his mind was active. Possibly a tunnel connected from the Abbey?

Where was water to be found in such an emergency? "We collect terrace water in a cistern under the tower," the monk said.

Gian stared out to sea. There were no ships, none of those ships he had seen departing Genoa harbour. It was the navigational use of this tall tower that intrigued him most. Knowing with precision where you were on the open seas had been a challenge for sailors since humans first took to the oceans. Knowing where you were, or else risking shipwreck. Always needing certainty and accuracy. This world always needed accuracy and truth.

This young mechanick understood that real facts came from measurement and careful observation, careful recording. For him, the pirate stories didn't have particular interest. Pirates were for uncivilised people living far from here.

After they inspected the tower, Leo took the Abbey boat to Camogli, promising Gian he would wait at Camogli tavern at noon on an appointed Thursday in a few weeks.

—

Gian's task was to attend and learn everything.

Wednesdays at the Abbey were devoted to ancient studies. "Ptolemy's motion of the planets is knowledge we have studied for many centuries," explained Professor Miguel. "It describes how the stars and planets move across the skies and around the Earth."

Gian knew his astronomy. Whenever Uncle Antonio could obtain a book for him, he read. He knew Ptolemy's motions were problematic, and had been for two thousand years. Planets that could sometimes go backwards? How could there be some simpler explanation for predicting where all five planets were at some date and time? Knowing the positions of the planets and stars was as important as birth dates for astrologers to make sound predictions.

Astrology Antonio had no time for, but it was Gian's first love. At the Jesuit College in Genoa, last year, one professor had given lessons in astrology. Those classes were held outside of proper class times, as the Jesuits were not comfortable with astrology being taught in their classes. But Gian was enthralled. Many of the wealthy and important



Cassini's Vision

people of Genoa, and some Popes in Rome, believed in the astrology. It served well those who had power. Gian had little power in his life yet.

—

The Professor arrived at class one Thursday with an unexpected guest teacher, one Father Battista, a Jesuit. Battista carried a long tubular instrument to demonstrate to the students. A "telescope" he termed it, and none of the boys had seen such a device. Using two glass lenses, ground into shape by hand after hours of work, the telescope could make distant objects appear larger to the eye.

Gian Cassini insisted on making a close inspection of the telescope, and the priest showed him how he could prise the lenses from the tube. All the details he could find, Gian sketched to a piece of paper. Battista explained what he had been able to understand about the lenses. "Optics", he called them. From Latin, easy.

The class hauled the telescope from the Abbey building uphill to the watchtower and up its steps, and they took turns to balance it over the balustrade to view the limited patch of faraway coastline and a tiny sailboat out to sea. The boat was looking a little larger, but it was somewhat fuzzy and distorted.

Father Battista had to hurry away before the afternoon was late. He would stay at Genoa for the night and start towards Florence in the morning, to return the telescope there to a Signor Galilei. The boys helped drag a sailboat from its cavernous tunnel under the Abbey, across the sand to the edge of the water. Two monks walked down with oars, and in the mild wind the three clerics began the slow sail East towards Camogli.

Young Giovanni Cassini had a new project—"optics". A telescope that could enlarge what he saw. Planets in the night sky that looked bigger. Astrology with more accuracy in observing the planets and the stars. He would make a telescope, and he would make it work better.

—

Against the rules, Gian on some mornings crept out of the Abbey to sit at the water's edge at dawn. He knew the narrow passage that led to the arches, the boat caves, beneath the central building. It was dark.

It was no beach to watch the rising Sun, but it was still a romance to be listening to the quiet water lapping as the faint golden light emerged from the black of the predawn.

No lights were on yet at the Abbey behind.

The light was still pale, the wind was slight. As Gian sat on the sand looking out to sea, he watched the incoming white froth on the water. The salty and seaweedy air smells were aggressive, and no one else would choose to be here.

A cloth was wrapped across his eyes, and his contemplation was shattered. A rough hand on his mouth stifled any sound he could have made.

"Make no noise, you infidel."

The intruder jerked the boy's head, and Gian forced a nod. The cloth relaxed. A second man stood in front brandishing a long blade.

"Tell us where inside is the Christian chapel? We need to know."

The brigand put his knife to the boy's throat. Gian choked and closed his eyes. The blade stung, he spluttered, and then he saw drops of dark when the sword was drawn back.

"How do you speak Italian?" he gasped. Bide for time.

"My mother was Italian," said the Moor. "My father took her from near here as a slave many years ago. Then he got soft-hearted. But stop talking. Where is the gold of the chapel? Point it to me."

                    Cassini's Vision

The dawn Angelus bell rang out from the Abbey, from the spire atop the chapel. Candle lights appeared at several of the monks' cell windows.

"Nahn muta'akhirun jiddaan," whispered the Italianate Moor to his colleague. "By Allah, we are too late. We go. But we will return."

With not a sound, the two amateur pirates ran across the stony sand, and pushed their boat away to row around the short rocky point of the inlet.

—

The day studies were finished and it was dusk. Gian wandered alone behind the Abbey near the abrupt slopes of the mountain range. From here rear accesses led into the kitchen, and some cut wood was stockpiled, but otherwise little space remained other than for one person walking. A foot track led away from the master building to a separate small barn mostly hidden by trees.

Behind a dense shrub against the ancient stone wall of the barn, Gian noticed through the foliage something different in the wall surface. Scrambling into the tight space past the shrub, he found that what he had seen was an old wooden door, strong and braced with iron straps, but appearing to be not opened for a long time.

Checking he was alone, he crouched and cleared away the dirt and rocks that stopped the door swinging outwards. It was to no avail, as an old lock was still holding the door secure. He found a rock and struck the lock.

The day was darkening. Gian prised the door open to still barely ajar. All was well hidden behind the disguising shrubbery. He squeezed inside and waited until his eyes accommodated. It was a tiny chamber, a pace and a half each side, about five palmi, but there was an opening on his left side, leading into the black. The place smelled of old carcass, and a child-sized skeleton lay propped against the right wall, untidy, stinky.

His courage faltered. Gian crawled back out and closed the door.

Two dawns later he returned, with an accomplice, a fellow student. The monks were in chapel. Gian and Paolo carried oil torches, but lit them only when inside the chamber, using the tiny lamp flame they had brought.

The horror of the skeleton was apparent now in the torchlight. Paolo wanted to leave.

"No. Let's go slow."

The doorway to the left was the start of stone steps leading downwards.

Their torches flamed and cast moving shadows, but the two adventurers crept down the steps into a crypt. The air was dank, and now filling with smoke from the torches. Niches in one wall were likely ancient burials. Gian refused to look at those past his first glance. Otherwise, the room stored junk—decaying books, art frames, kitchen pots.

"And a clock."

"Clock? Where?"

At some distance away in the blackness, Gian could hear only the faint sound of water dripping.

"Can't you see it? Over there." In the poor light Paolo pointed with his crooked finger.

"That's old."

"So is everything down here!"

That was enough.

Taking nothing, they left and closed the door.

That clock. He should have taken a close look. An abandoned clock. No one he knew owned a clock. This should be his clock.

—

By four weeks later, the same clock had a fresh hiding place in Gian's room. He must get it out of here soon, move it to Genoa before it was discovered.

Commandment 7. Non furtum facies. Non rubare. Thou shalt not steal. Thou shalt NOT STEAL.

So far, he had improvised a primitive tool to allow him to dismantle and then reassemble the clock frame and its workings. Every part and the way it fitted with all the others he had studied and measured closely, and he had sketched and described it in detail in his personal workbook.

The clock had a broken gut string. That must wait until he had the old device back home.

Next week he would make his last dismantling, and wrap the parts for smuggling home that Thursday. That was when the Abbey boat would make its scheduled student ferry run to Camogli.

A few days ago, he had checked the crypt doorway yet again. Someone had re-locked the door and tamped the soil at the foot of the door to appear as though no one had disturbed it in years.

—

"Since our talk last month, Giovanni, on your last visit back home, I have made more enquiries for you. Your Signor Galilei is Galileo Galilei, and he lives in Florence. This much you already know.

"The man is quite famous there, but now he's old. This telescope you saw was an object that Galilei himself invented some decades ago. He's had many scandals in his life and his work, and Rome has imprisoned him in his home for some years now, because his telescope has led him to opinions that are not acceptable. But this Galilei has studied and written on many new subjects, and he has a strong reputation."

"How can it be that looking at something with better vision can be a bad thing?"

"That I can't say. I don't understand that either."

"Uncle Antonio, will you take me to see Signor Galilei?"

—

Antonio agreed. The boy was old enough to profit from such a trip. Childhood was drawing to its close, and Giovanni to Antonio was as a true son.

The job of Public Notary placed Antonio in the business company of many of the noble and wealthy citizens of Genoa and the surrounding regions. All substantial commercial and legal dealings needed notary services for registration and authentication. Antonio had many friends from whom he could call in favours.

He called Gian to make arrangements. The trip had developed into a grander tour. "I have business connections in other cities that can profit by a visit in the next month or two. Bologna has tasks, and also Venice. And so, Gian, you will come with me, and after I transact my business, I will show you Florence and then Venice.

"Your Signor Galilei in Florence is ailing, but I have told him of your interests, and he has sent me a message that he would be pleased to see you. He is offering you a gift deserving considerable gratitude in good time."

"Fine. I will remember."

"For myself, I have a request for you as well. Between now and when we can depart, I want you to study what you can about those cities. We are not merely taking a holiday. What are they noted for? Who are their heroes? What is their business, their function, their money and trade, their religious affiliations?

"For a start, Gian, what do you know of Venice?"

"That it is a city of licentiousness and sin and carnival, of defiance against the Pope, and of effortless wealth from its shipping trade. It is a competitor of our Genoa."

"Possibly, Gian. However, it may have a morality that is not what you expect. And its wealth may not be so unearned. Not everything is as simple as it looks.

"Next, Bologna, what do you know?"

"That it's a city of old colleges. Pure learning."

"Hmm. We need to show you the place where they carve up dead humans. Plain learning perhaps isn't what you understand either."

"Oh dear, but get me to Florence before the old Signor dies."

Antonio Crovese had share ownership in four horses kept a little out of town in a stables and agistment cooperative property. Short requests for a couple of horses were as easy as a two-hour messenger trip to fetch the horses to town.

"I will, I promise. In some weeks' time. For long journeying I need a few weeks to arrange horses. We need to be back well before Easter, and Rome changed the Easter date again this year.

"We'll get into Florence, and we will see Signor Galilei. But when we are in Florence, we should see there the grandest art you will ever find. At Florence, you might think on whence comes the wealth that pays for that profligate art. What contracts and pacts are written between the owners of that art and the producers, between the court and the artists? Do they sell souls or money, power or fame, passion or only labour? Perhaps you think they are just trading in God and religion."

—

Christmas in Europe is a cold time. The fields yield little, and the animals need sheltering. By tradition, the food was mostly what had been preserved when the climate was more productive. It was a time of surviving, a time of hardship.

The meal and festivity of Christmas Day, however, carried a strong element of defiance. The birth of the Christ child was a new beginning, a happiness, an optimism. Everyone ignored that it was mid-winter. There was an abundance of delicious food, an excess. All enjoyed being with their families, and forgave slights.

Genoa's climate was milder and more kindly than much of inland and northerly Europe, but Christmas was still celebrated with similar spirit.

Thirty-six of Antonio's family, most now returned from early Mass, were ready to enjoy the foods laid out on the refectory table. All had dressed for Christmas, but some were of wealthy households and some were less well off. All were planning to eat, and eat.

A minstrel with a fiddle sat himself in the corner of the room preparing for merriment.

On the tables were sweetcakes and marzipans and small breads of many types. For the past half hour, the arriving guests had stood and mingled, and had been eating straight from the plates already on the tables. Some moved to the fire to be warm.

Leo, Antonio's assistant, now cleared the crowd from near the tables.

A copper pan arrived filled with a steaming mashed potato with chopped raw onion, all heavy with pepper and spices and butter. Servants delivered two trays from the kitchen loaded with heaped slices of roast beef that had been long hours on the spit. One more tray had a turkey, a "New World" bird, carved into pieces, but cleverly arranged back on the tray pinned and assembled again to the shape of the big bird. Around the turkey were pieces of a half-dozen carved roasted fowl. Dishes of cold and green vegetables arrived last.

All were still hungry. All were eyeing with anticipation the feast on the laden trestles, that banquet with such aromas filling the room.

Jugs of several wines were placed along the trestles.

Antonio waved the crowd back to the tables, and left Leo to assign seating places.

Fussy mothers were giving confused youngsters fast impromptu instructions in modern table manners, on how to use the unfamiliar fork instead of knife points or fingers to pick up their food, and how not to wipe their hands on the cloth on the trestle tables, even to spit behind them if they needed, but not forward onto the table.

Antonio made the brief welcomes and the Christmas wishes, and invited all to eat.

By an hour later many were again standing and mixing. Young Gian stood with the other guests watching and listening to the antics of the minstrel, who had played through all the meal. Gian had not noticed Celia come up behind him.

"Gian, what's inside a clock?"

He startled. And he couldn't mistake the second part of the transaction; Celia's breast had pressed into his back. It was gentle and it was quick.

How could she know of his clock? The clock was still in pieces hidden in his room. He was blushing.

"The clock?"

"A clock. Any clock."

He breathed.

"My parents have bought a clock. I want to know why it works, even while no one watches. I could pretend a spirit lives in there, but I know that can't be. You see into things better than other boys, so I'm asking you. Come outside to the garden and tell me about clocks."

Antonio observed, but he didn't let on. He knew a little of this one, his cousin's daughter. Once he had visited her amateur artwork shop and heard her there reading poetry. He knew that this young girl with the wild reputation had savvy and promise. And fire.

Antonio had eaten well, and had enjoyed his share of the fine wine. The Christmas gathering of the family had unfolded as well as such tricky feast days might.

Gian and his garden conspirator returned from the cold after a few minutes into the dining hall.

The minstrel was still performing. Antonio listened for a while, and then left the room for a moment, returning with an older violin. He clapped for attention. "Josefo is handling his fiddle well, do we all agree?"

He held aloft his violin. "Let's see how Josefo can make this little old lady sing. She's an Andrea Amati made a hundred years ago just this year, in Cremona, and Cremona is the violin capital of all Europe. Tune her up, Josefo, and you have thirty minutes to impress us all. Let's do Christmas. Let's do it well."

# Florence

Tired and sore, they arrived from Lucca into Florence on horseback. The horse track had been damp, and the smell of horse dung had lost its appeal.

"Signor Galilei does not take visitors," insisted the guard at the door.

"But we are friends. From afar. He is expecting us this week."

Grudgingly, the guard allowed them to enter. Galilei's old attendant came down and escorted them in.

Old Galilei had known they would be visiting. "Ferodo, arrange accommodation and meals for my friends. Organise them for three nights. And see to their horses, please."

Ferodo brought them water for washing. Then they ate well, and they slept long.

The visitors gathered at mid-morning in Galilei's study. Ferodo had settled the Signor into a comfortable seat, and had covered his legs with a blanket.

"First you must tell me why you have come to visit me. You have seen I am guarded, and taking visitors is not easy."

"My nephew begged me to see you. He has shown a recent and passionate need to find and use a telescope. In his college at Genoa, he saw one of your telescopes. A visiting lecturer had demonstrated it to the class, one Jesuit Father Battista, and he credited the invention and the making of it to you."

"Ah, no I did not invent the spyglass. The first I learned of it was from a traveller from Flanders in the Netherlands, where he had seen one exhibited in the laboratory of a local spectacle maker. That spectacles seller found his children using two discarded lenses to make distant things seem nearer and bigger."

"You obtained a telescope from the Netherlands?"

"No, I just thought for a long time on the concept. I knew only that he used two lenses. So I went back six hundred years to read Abu al-Hasan's Book of Optics, and I experimented until I worked out how to make my own. Ferodo can bring in the telescope Gian would have seen in Genoa. That was my third attempt, and each version I try to make better than the previous. Over the years I have now ground many lenses, and it's tedious and exacting. I am seeking to test and prove the best mathematic shape for the lens, because merely spherical curving is not good enough. And yet grinding by hand to even a spherical accuracy is so difficult!"

Gian produced his paper sketch from college. The detail he had recorded he now described to Galilei, who nodded with pleasure.

"I would like," said the old man, "that you would tell me your story, Giovanni. Tell me of your family and of your schooldays. What things interest you, what are your passions? In your own words, why did you want to come so far to see me, a frail man whose work is done?"

So, Galilei listened to Gian's story. A boy story. An enthusiast's story. A story of passion and ambition.

And then a silence fell.

"Giovanni, do you play any music? All my life I have played the lute. Ferodo, bring me my lute."

He played a few notes.

"If I hit the lute string hard, it plays a loud note. If I hit it gently, it plays the same note, but softly. On a lute, we use a longer string if we want a lower note. Or you can also raise the note by tightening the string. As an inquisitive musician, and applying my mathematical studies, I learned that for any given string, the note depends on the square root of the tension.

"Mathematics is the language or the set of rules that describes the things in our world. Learn this, Giovanni."

Mathematics? Oh.

"It was not I who discovered the rules behind my lute string; Pythagoras did, two thousand years ago. And during those two thousand years, no one has bothered to keep asking why that is so.

"But what were those rules? And so, I put different weights on different strings and I tested with them. I watched other examples of objects suspended in several ways, fixed and free."

He paused.

"One day I was attending Holy Mass in the Cathedral at Pisa when I noticed a curious thing. Many chandeliers hung from the ceiling, and sometimes when the door opened a gust of wind would start them swaying. Their sway was much slower than the vibrations in my lute string, but still I would by instinct watch them, measure them in my head. Like my loud lute notes and the soft ones, the swaying lamps, swinging wild or gently, large arc or small, nevertheless made the same count of swings over a time. I confess to bringing a sand timer into Church sometimes to be sure I was not mistaken."

He waved to Ferodo. Ferodo understood, and brought across a stand with a hanging ball on a rope.

"A pendulum—that's what I call it. You should observe for yourself what I say."

Gian played with the pendulum, counted the swings with the timer, and indeed Galilei's claim appeared to be correct.

"Now shorten the length of the device. Draw up the rope and re-clamp it. See it swings faster? But Gian, how can we predict precisely how much faster than before?"

Cassini adjusted, swung, tested Galilei's pendulum, and then shook his head.

"That's the task of observation and mathematics," said the old man.

"I have some regrets in my life," he continued. "My guess is every old man will have some. Long ago I published my pendulum observations, and the mathematical rules a pendulum follows. It was about forty years ago. But I regret I had never seen a practical way until recently for using my pendulum. My son Vincenzo has been helping me. We have a design, but we still don't have it working. Now is too late."

"I can see your published work on the pendulum, Signor Galilei?" asked Gian.

"But yes. Take a copy home with you."

Gian grinned. Galilei couldn't see, but he could hear the meaning of the silence.

"And the name everyone knows me by is just Galileo. For you also, call me Galileo.

"One more thing Giovanni, Gian. On the table are two lenses. They are for you."

—

Galileo did not appear on the second morning. Ferodo reported he was indisposed.

After lunchtime, Ferodo fetched them to the old man's room. He was sleeping again, so they waited. Gian recalled from yesterday that smell in this room, musty, stale, old man smell. Smell of ill-health.

They were offered Ethiopian coffee. To Gian, it was unfamiliar and not to his taste. Galilei awoke and smiled, as only the blind can smile.

"Today I will talk with your Uncle. I trust your Uncle. But Gian, stay with us and listen and learn.

"Antonio, I thank you most sincerely for coming to my home. Particularly I am honoured you bring your talented nephew to meet me and share the passion that for me is now failing.

"My trusted friends are now few. As is obvious, I am a prisoner, even in my own house. And if I were free, my health now makes walking a problem. My time is finished.

"I have learned of your reputation in Genoa, Signor Crovese. Last month I confess I had Ferodo make enquiries. I accept you as a man of influence and of honour.

"At this late time, I am sharing my long tale with only a few I can trust. So then perhaps the saga may be remembered or recorded, and not consigned to oblivion and irrelevance. I have seen so much that no one ever knew or dreamed before.

"I am old, and I'm breaking, Crovese."

He fell silent a while.

"Antonio, I am pleased your nephew has taken a complete copy of my treatise on the pendulum. It's a rather old work. Many times I have thought of revisiting that work, of making it useful. Encourage your boy. Tell him it's time." He coughed and managed a chuckle.

"The biggest mistake I ever made was not a mistake of observation or of fact—and of those mistakes there have been plenty—or even of incautiously publishing my work. Where I misjudged was in leaving Padua many years ago and coming to live and work here in Florence. I should still be a free man, and my findings would stand respected and be marvelled at. It would be carried into the future by new minds, new passion, with freedom to regard with honesty God's awesome universe.

"Antonio, I have tried to love the great Lord, and I have wanted to be an honest man, honest to my beliefs. It is hard, because what I believe to be sincere work has brought such conflict from His holy Church," he said.

"My parents were poor." A story was starting.

"There was no inheritance coming to me, I could see that, so I needed early to find a profession to support my life.

I could be either a competent artist or a good musician, I decided. Either of those two might have made me a living. I played the lute well, for one thing.

"But my parents wished I should study medicine, which included Latin and Greek and astrology. So I took up medicine at my University of Pisa. That medicine, I never finished it. I became enthralled with the geometries of Euclid, and mathematics, and natural things of every kind.

"Many of my investigations made me question the teachings of Aristotle, ideas accepted for two thousand years and held as precious by my superiors. However, where I could prove my conclusions by my recorded observations, Aristotle could not prove his. That was unfortunate! The University threw me out. I was a problem.

"After I documented my discoveries on the time invariance of the pendulum, then I became more noticed. The same University appointed me as its Professor of Mathematics. I was twenty-five.

"Again I annoyed them when I showed how Aristotle's claim was wrong that heavier objects fall faster. Things I dropped over the side of the leaning tower proved I was correct. I was a rebel, questioning ancient and non-negotiable dogma on how the world worked. I was making more enemies.

"Then I offended the port governor, a de Medici indeed, by embarrassing him about his pump designs to drain the dock. Because I was right: it wouldn't work and it didn't work. But I was arrogant. I had no welcome left in Pisa.

"I still had some friends, and Padua made me Mathematics Professor. Youth was still on my side. In Padua, I flourished. I had jumped north from the suspicious de Medici lands of Florence and Pisa whose Roman allegiances vacillated wildly. I jumped past Bologna in the Papal States where the Inquisition was always a threat. And I landed in Padua up in the Veneto region. In all that State of Venice, philosophers like me were protected from Rome and the

Inquisition by the strong influence of that independent priest Fra Paolo Sarpi.

"Venice is another country entirely, rebellious, non-conforming, licentious even. The whole spectrum of Natural Philosophy was open for me. I was free. I could call it Science. I researched. I observed. I documented. I studied the mathematics underlying so many natural things. And the crowds of students and private pupils were a pride to me. Ferodo joined me those many years ago, and he has since been my skilled maker of countless experiment machines."

Gian was rapt. A lifetime of new experiments and discoveries—complete with a competent assistant, pupils, and an income.

The old man stayed silent a long time.

"It was in Padua that I made my first telescope. My version of telescope worked much better than the Flanders report had indicated for what the Dutch called their 'perspective glass'. Rumours about mine spread into Venice. The full Senate in Venice summoned me to appear. Together the city Fathers took my telescope up to a high tower in the city and gazed through it to see what approaching ships might be still far away on the horizon, not yet visible by naked eye. Venice is a trading port and it has had to fight many sea battles. The significance of hours of extra notice of incoming ships was obvious. They obliged me to make several telescopes for the business people of Venice. Only for Venice.

"In the long run, the telescope has been my enemy. My interest became pointing it to the heavens, and the detail I saw made clear that Mister Copernicus with no spyglass was indeed right a hundred years ago. Our Earth does circle the Sun, and the other planets do too. Indeed, Earth must itself be a planet. I saw things that my mind for a long time opposed. One of our planets has four of its own smaller planets circling it. Long ago I discovered those. The mathematics is challenging, but the facts are clear to see."

Gian knew this was outright heresy. It could not be true. The man was deluded.

"I did not publish these discoveries. It was too dangerous. Only some of my students knew.

"By now I had established a wide reputation. The Venice shipyard complex, the Arsenal, commissioned me to study its whole operation, how to make shipbuilding and provisioning much faster, how to guarantee every item going aboard was of the highest quality, and how to ensure supply of every material and labour was available at the correct time. My huge report is still their reference book. You did visit the Arsenal, Gian?"

"Not yet. Next week we travel to Venice."

"Study it. Venice functions by mathematics and precision and timing."

Galilei turned his head back towards Antonio.

"Well now, after eighteen years, Tuscany invited me back. I could go back home. All could be forgiven. My salary would increase beyond believing. They appointed me Resident Mathematician and Personal Philosopher to the Grand Duke of Tuscany in Florence, de Medici country. I was to be a person who could give glory and prestige to the Grand Duke's court. Oh, what a misjudgement!"

Ferodo straightened his master's coverings.

"Before my story continues to Florence, I must explain my family. I have not married, but I did have a mistress in Padua, Marina, who was from Venice. Marina and I had three children, but her origins did not fit with the University world I lived in. In Padua, in all the Veneto region, for a busy and prosperous man to enjoy his mistress is a trifling misdemeanour.

"When I returned to Florence, Marina went back to her Venice, and I am happy to know she married well and contentedly a couple of years later. Her husband remains a friend of mine. My children from Marina belonged to me, and moved to Florence with me.

                                    Cassini's Vision

"Marina I loved with a wonderful fondness, and as an old man, I still grieve without end that I could not provide for her the lasting happiness she deserved. The Venice world is different. Venice and Padua might cope with the irregular life we led there, but the critical and prim Florence world would never," he said.

"Antonio, the children were illegitimate. My two daughters had no prospects for marriage. Three years after I moved to Florence, when they were thirteen and eleven, I paid their dowries and placed them both into the Franciscan Convent of St Matthew at Arcetri near Florence. All their lives they have lived there as nuns. I trust that my God sees I have served my daughters well. My third child, Vincenzo, I paid to have declared a legitimate son and heir."

Ferodo brought refreshments, and Galileo rested.

"In Florence," Galileo resumed, "I returned to studying the skies.

"And that's when Rome pronounced its formal edict. They declared finally that all the Sun-centred theory of Copernicus from last century was heretical. But my observations and my class lectures had been in support of Copernicus' results, and Rome called me to defend my work. A respectful and friendly Pope Paul V exonerated me.

"Here is where I erred again. Paul's successor Urban VIII was also my friend, I had assumed. And so ten years ago I dared to publish more of my writings. My statements didn't actually claim outright as Copernicus did that Earth circled the Sun, but they did discuss the theory.

"The Inquisition called me to Rome again. My Grand Duke stuck by me and appealed for clemency, but it was to no avail. In the Inquisition's great hall I knelt before the Cardinals, and they issued me with a legal charge of heresy against Holy Writ. 'Vehemently suspected of heresy,' was how they labelled it.

"I was a frail man, Antonio. They were ready to torture me. I surrendered," he said.

"I put my hands on the Bible, and I solemnly renounced my heresies and my depravity. I read aloud in detail the things I repudiated forever, that the Sun could be the centre in our universe, and all the rest. They commuted my punishment to life restraint in my house. They took my recantation statements to Florence and read them to all my students and colleagues."

Galileo stayed silent a while. He closed his eyes.

"Had I stayed in Padua, I would have been remote from the machinations of Rome."

Galileo slept again. They stayed with him. Gian was frightened.

Galileo opened his eyes. "Young Cassini, you are a diligent observer, and passionate. You have an outstanding future if only you are brave enough to grasp it. Always remember, what you can ever see is never the whole truth. Something more is always there. Keep looking for more truth. Let this old man tell you: you must be courageous, because all the forces in our world want us never to reach the truth. Sit near me."

He placed his hand out and found Gian's arm, and he spoke carefully to him. Gian nodded, by instinct.

Suddenly, the bulky door swung open and Ferodo stumbled in. The door guard was holding and jostling him.

"What's afoot?" called Galileo.

"Signor, I'm sorry." Ferodo's face was bruised and his jacket was torn. "The guard is here, Signor. Sorry, Signor."

"I instructed you never to come inside my home," shouted Galileo to the guard. "What is the meaning of this?"

"My orders are also that you should not have visitors. I have been tolerant many times, because I know you are a distinguished man. But Ferodo tells me your discussions these days are on forbidden things. Your guests must leave. I should be reporting these breaches of your confinement."

"But you won't. I feed you, and your family."

"Then these people must depart at once."

"Very well. Tomorrow they can leave. For now, I shall sleep. You all may leave me."

—

Ferodo placated the Roman guard. He managed to find two big jugs of new season wine that Galilei's elder convent daughter had sent as a Christmas gift to her old father and her brother Vincenzo. But Vincenzo was abroad, and Galilei was no longer inclined to enjoy his wine. Ferodo was concerned it should be used before spoiling. So the bribe was enough to buy one more day's stay for the visitors.

Ferodo made leave of his master for the afternoon, satisfied the old fellow was safe for a few hours.

The three made their way to the area of city government near the Palazzo Vecchio, and came into the Piazza della Signoria. In pride of place in the square was a marble statue three times the height of a mere living human. This spectacular sculpture was the masterwork of Michelangelo, carved more than a century before. This was David, known across Europe, the most famous statue in the world.

In the same square, five all-day market stands were trading. Across the other side several tables were set out, and patrons were sitting, watching, and drinking their wines or their teas. Or just sitting.

It was the statue that held unchallenged dominance. For ten minutes they stood in silence, consigning the enormity and awe of the sculpture to that memory that preserves superb life moments.

A young man stood up from one of the tables and approached them. Ferodo greeted him as a friend, as one he had been patiently expecting.

"Antonio, I wish you to meet a dear friend. This is Signor Salvator Rosa. My master has plotted that you should meet. Salvator Rosa, Antonio Crovese, and his nephew Giovanni."

The four men sat again at Rosa's table. The afternoon was cool.

"Wine, Signors?"

"For us all a warmed pomegranate tea would be excellent," replied Rosa.

"Our speciality, a splendid choice, Signor."

"One can't ever tire of looking at David," said Rosa. "The detail, the human realities."

The aggressive nakedness, thought Gian. Well, it was confronting.

"The young man David in his prime readying his strength. David making ready to tackle the mighty warrior, a fighter bigger than him, an enemy of his people, the oppressor no one knew how to best. It's a study in meditation, on personal confidence, as much as it is about muscles and posture and veins. We need to take a look beyond the obvious. Where are David's eyes looking? This sculpture is about mind. The battle is still to be fought."

A light rain started to fall, and the air smelled of that rain, fresh.

Salvator Rosa hurried them to the Galleria dell'Accademia with its immense collection of beautiful artwork. His opinions were unorthodox and unapologetic.

Rosa was in exile, working in Florence because he had made powerful enemies in Rome where he had earlier achieved his first fame and some small fortune.

They moved then to a modest studio across town that Rosa called his *Accademia dei Percossi*, the Academy of the Stricken, a boast on his rebelliousness and his opponents.

"This studio is all I can afford here," he complained limply. "I want space to do grand canvases of immense scenes. One day ..."

It was plain, nevertheless, that his studio was the headquarters salon for a motley band of poets, painters and playwrights, artistic people all of them, all with opinions and attitude.

"They warn against me here," he said. "They warn 'Don't associate with the wild one Rosa.' But I do have a few pupils."

As they parted late in the afternoon, Antonio thanked their guide. "Salvator, your insights have been a pleasure to share. Thank you for giving your time so heartily."

"My pleasure. And," he said, glancing to Ferodo, "my primary mission today has been to introduce young Gian, more than your good self, to our world of art, its foibles, its politics, and its foolish wealth." He gave Ferodo a light friendly punch to the arm.

—

"Tomorrow we ride to Bologna. A handsome city, set in a district they call La Grassa, the fat and fertile place. I have some contract paperwork to check with a Count, a Senator in Bologna. Otherwise, we have a couple of days to look around. It's a grand old city. I know you wish now to reach Venice, but Bologna is on our way to Venice."

Antonio arranged three nights stay in a comfortable inn at the outskirts of the city.

The promised Anatomy Theatre was not operating on the few days they were visiting. However, Antonio's client, one wealthy Marquis Malvasia, was pleased to take them through the premises for a private inspection.

"We have had an Anatomy Theatre for a long time, but it's only two years ago we finished building this new one."

Inside, the amphitheatre was all fitted out in carved cedar, with steep seating tiered up the rear walls. Sculptures of the ancient physicians starting with Hippocrates stood in alcoves around the walls. In the ceiling, a carved Apollo and an angel watched all that happened below. The astrological zodiac circled them.

Low at the centre, commanding most of the attention, was the marble table for the corpse. Behind the dissection table, the teacher's chair stood, elevated, and from here the professor held court. Two male statues were each side of the professor, skin stripped off and muscles on view.

Torches and candles were the primary lighting, most at the foot and head of the body, but today only some were lit.

"The medical school has classes here, but during Carnival, the theatre holds public dissections daily for two weeks. Cushions and damask will decorate the room. Students, city officials, and women dressed in high fashion and some in masks will come by day, and return at night to the balls and antics of Carnival."

"It's quite a major ceremony," the Marquis continued. "The professor guides a broad discussion about general medicine, philosophy and observable anatomy, and he steps down at times to indicate parts on the cadaver. He might often concentrate the day's discussion upon one particular body organ. Over the two weeks, the whole body can thus be covered. And his assistants will have prepared the bodies for easy demonstration."

"Bodies? Plural?"

"Well, after a few days, we bring in a fresher corpse."

Gian thought a while. "Signor Malvasia, who are the corpses? Where do the bodies come from?"

Antonio shook his head and closed his eyes.

"We are well supplied," said the Marquis, "I assure you. The poor who have no money to be buried can be a theatre corpse, as can executed criminals. However, they need to come from at least thirty miles away from Bologna."

"It won't ever be me?"

# Venice

**"N**o one has ever conquered Venice," Uncle Antonio had explained while they ate breakfast before riding. "Venice is the Serenissima, the imperturbable. Or Venetia la Ricca, the rich. The Venetians believe themselves the survivors of the last fleeing Romans of the fifth century, and therefore they are the true Romans, they think. And though it has long been Catholic, it has kept the Papal authority at arm's length. It has never entertained the Protestant religions, either. Venice has been incredibly wealthy and self-assured for centuries, although it is less so now. It still has a reputation for licence and libertinism, and gambling dens."

They continued to journey in the mainland, and they rode later in the day towards Fusina. Fusina had many stables to cater for such travellers, and lodging for resting before proceeding by barge to Venice.

Antonio now rode alongside Gian. "This month is Venice masquerading season, and it will be party time, but not the full Carnival. The theatres will be open, concerts and people in fancy dress will be everywhere. We have a lot to see."

They checked into the Fusina lodgings.

Slept and refreshed, they took a horse-drawn barge to themselves, to avoid the motley throng of ruffians on the bigger boats. Floating along the Brenta, they watched palatial villas and stately gardens pass them slowly on the banks.

As the river opened out, they left the horses behind, and they were rowed across the shallow sea called La Laguna. Slowly, slowly across the sea, the buildings and towers of a whole city moved in from the morning mist before them.

"See the city has no walls, Gian."

Every Italian city boasted fortifications. Venice was defended by water only, the shallowness and the canal structure. It had proven impregnable.

They could see no mighty ships, only many smaller boats. What lay at anchor here were not ships but stately buildings of a city. A city of stone and gleaming marble, floating on the sea.

The two stepped ashore, and took only their leather luggage bags with them. They had stored some things in Fusina. Antonio negotiated with a gondolier to take them to their lodging.

"It stinks," called Gian. A stench rose out of the canal waters. It was inescapable. Drains were not a possibility. The feeble tides must be the only way the city cleaned itself. How many days were they planning to stay in this smelly place?

Their gondola, black like all the rest, passed church after church, San Sebastian, the Angel Rafael, under footbridges, past intersections, and they came out after a time into a much broader waterway with more and bigger boats.

"The Grand Canal."

Gondolas aplenty plied their traffic, and many waited at the public wharves. Each gondola would seat six or more, and a thick black cloth canopy was set above the heads of all passengers.

The grandest of the bridges spanned the Grand Canal. The immense single higher-clearance arch in white marble was supporting covered pedestrian ramps, fine smaller arches, and room for shops. This was the iconic and magnificent Rialto Bridge. They would come back.

They glided under the Rialto and then turned right onto one other narrow canal to be let out at their accommodation. From the gondola they stepped onto the ledge at the house door. The water came to the door.

The house was enormous and lavish. Antonio's Venice colleague Bernardo lived here, entertained here, staged trade negotiations here. It had visitor quarters for business contacts, friends, emissaries, and by reputation even foreign royalty on occasions. Three gondolas were tied up alongside.

They were dined suitably, and Antonio and Bernado retired to a meeting room for much of the afternoon.

Young Cassini slipped out the rear doorway to explore the laneways behind the mansion. These were not passable streets as in any other city, not enough passage for a cart of any size. Most of the alleys were called Calle. All were winding and narrow, sometimes not one pace wide. The walkways crossed the many narrow canals on stone arched footbridges. Venice must have a huge number of these bridges.

And under these arches passed countless gondolas. The principal thoroughfares of Venice, the front aspect of all its palaces, mansions and tenements, were the canals, not the alleys. The winding streets were the secondary inter-connectors only. For Gian the foreigner, the whole layout was confusing. How did his Uncle know all these cities?

But return safely Gian did. Antonio was ready to take a walk to St Mark's Piazza; they would have their evening meal out. The Piazza was only two canal bridges away. In that short stroll, they passed nevertheless silk shops, book shops, an apothecary, shops with carnival masks and windows displaying gold clothing. One shop sold naught but its famous treacle. A tavern beside one canal was becoming noisy and the afternoon was not yet done. Two young women wearing yellow scarves loitered nearby.

"It's a signal. Keep watching."

Down one alley was a barely disguised brothel, with its wares and services listed and prostitutes seen waiting inside. One wore a mask and had bare breasts.

"Puttana. No licence. And wearing a mask, she is assumed at law to be at play," said Antonio. "Venice even has a Bridge of Tits. The Ponte delle Tette." Gian hesitated to look to the girls, but Antonio was walking on.

"Interesting city: most brothels are licensed, with public prostitutes. A directory lists all their names and their prices, and more than fifteen thousand are on that list. When you pass, they will flirt and reveal a little for you."

My Uncle is obsessed. Where is all this leading?

"The better of the women, the true courtesans, are gracious and very beautiful, and they can entertain, sing, dance or be an interesting dinner escort. They dress lavishly, including embroidered hosiery and underwear, and silk brocade over. Men travel from afar to Venice to sample the elegance of its courtesans. Those women can be famous, much sought after, and rich, rich, rich. Their houses, though, you won't notice, because they are no different from the portly homes of the nobility, spacious and filled with gilt leather furnishings and sumptuous tapestries. They may support their own household of servants."

"All government-licensed?"

"Venice has many times lost many of its people to waves of the plague, because it is a port city. For a long time, the authorities have been afraid that too many of the young men preferred to sleep with other men, and the population regrowth was too slow. Therefore, they decided sodomy should be made evil and illegal. Brothels proliferated to retrain their menfolk. And the brothel tax is substantial."

"Oh. Then there are no male prostitutes?"

"Well yes, there are, the cicisbeo. They are to entertain the younger respectable wife while the husband visits his mistress. The cicisbeo might even be her accepted escort to dinners and public events. It all makes sense. No courtesan industry like this exists in the entire world."

Many men walked the Piazza who were tall and solemn, looking to be about important business, and not wanting to dally among lesser folk. The most noble all wore long black gowns, flying open, and a knitted cap of black. The cape covered a manly black suit, worn with stockings and garters and fine leather shoes.

"They are forbidden to talk with foreigners, and especially foreigners on business," said Antonio. "Venice is a jealous city. They could be punished as traitors."

Many of the women on the Piazza were tall-bodied also, but they stood taller by a head than any man. They wore tall shoes, ridiculously tall. Gian thought they might instead be stilts.

"Chopines," said Antonio. Each noblewoman walked with one or two older female assistants, placing her hands on their shoulders. These women were conspicuous, slow and to Gian quite absurd.

Where were the other young women of Venice, the normal folk?

"The unmarried stay off the streets. Except at Carnival or party time, and then in masks. Wait until dusk approaches. We may see some ordinary people. This is party week."

Indeed, nearing darkfall, more of the Venice people, high-born and not, were in the Piazza, alighting from their gondolas, promenading or strolling to their choice of dining or meeting. All the men, from the gentleman down to the sailors, wore a long outer garment, some coloured, green, scarlet, blue, crimson, but more often black. The men of prestige sported costly velvet or brocade or ermine, always ornate. Their sleeves fell close to the ground.

The pretty women among the wives were unashamed in what they showed, bare breasts and shoulders, and even uncovered backs. They were resplendent and bejewelled as best they could afford—maybe more than they could afford. The shoes still were often extraordinarily high and ungainly, and they needed support of husbands or friends. Thick layers of unnatural colour covered their faces, supposedly to be enhancing their beauty. Their hair was long and dyed white.

Then there were the other women, young, the unmarried, who appeared very different, well covered up in black, even over their heads.

—

Mid-morning, a gondola arrived to collect them. The boatman rowed them a long distance from their lodgings, through small apartments, past mansions, near warehouses. They pulled in to the steps of a well-appointed palace along a salubrious quiet canal.

Antonio and Gian, unsteady, stepped from the gondola, and were met at the foyer by Madame Anjelica. Uncle Antonio adjourned to the far lounge with Anjelica to discuss business, and he returned after counting out a sum of money for her. Then he was gone; he would return several hours later.

Giovanni Cassini, sixteen, was afraid. It was an initiation. For now, he was alone.

Mme Anjelica was slim and rather tall, and attractive. Certainly not French. Her age would be late 20s, Gian assessed. She was assured and she was in command, decidedly his superior.

The woman was not dressed like any of the noblewomen nor the courtesans they had seen in the square. No high shoes. No excessive and pinned up hair, little makeup. And no provocative display of exposed breast.

Her dress was a full-length shift of silk, and her womanly shape was completely covered, but beneath the light fabric he could see she was seductive, naked. The mid-length hair was a subdued red. Gian had never been close or involved before with any girl or woman quite so alluring in this alien way.

When she had him alone, she turned to him and said, "Young Gian, I want you to remember this one thing throughout your long life. With everything you think you know or believe, when you search further, something different is there to be learnt. Something wonderfully different. Today we will go looking."

Anjelica led him upstairs and to a room at the front of the premises, collecting as they entered two Venetian masks, handheld ones.

In the room, and waiting for them, were a man and a woman, each wearing a soft fitted mask, and again perhaps in their late twenties.

The walls were decorated, sumptuous, artistic. A fire was alight and the air was comfortable. A fragrance wafted through the room from a perfume bowl in one corner. The floor was tiled. On one side was a grand lounging platform, covered with furs and cushions. It was lower and more extended than any bed Gian had seen. On the other wall was a well-padded settee, big enough for two or perhaps three to lounge upon in comfort. Those two were the only pieces of furniture.

The two unknown guests stood at the high window frame looking out across the water, until Anjelica addressed them and introduced Gian. Their names were Veronica and Filippo. They remained then standing looking in towards Gian and Anjelica.

Mme Anjelica smiled. "I want to gaze at you," she said. "I want to see what a fine young man we have here." Still smiling and looking at his eyes, she loosened his trousers with practised hands, and had Gian step out of his underclothing.

"Beautiful," she cooed. She removed his shirt so that he was naked. "But look me in the eye."

Gian blushed a deep shade. His manhood lengthened immediately and rose a little. His shoulders were shivering with tension.

"Gian, that's a proud man's member. Let me walk around you and enjoy what I see."

Veronica and Filippo were watching too.

Anjelica came back to stand in front of him. She folded down the top of her dress to uncover her bosom.

Gian's experience of naked breasts was limited to seeing paintings in Antonio's house and in the museum. Not ever real flesh. Not ever close like this. Anjelica's breasts were small, and to a sixteen-year-old lad, so very exciting. The dark pink nipples were hardening buttons, protruding. The shivering grew more noticeable.

"May I?" the woman asked.

Gian stayed silent as both her hands moved with a tenderness to hold his rising penis.

"Now I want you to use your fingers to just touch my breasts. Feel the little points. Be gentle with me."

And so he did, as Anjelica and Veronica and Filippo watched him. His body shook, his face was burning, and his fingers moved across the magical small breasts of Anjelica.

"You enjoy doing that," she said softly. She began as well to caress his member.

Gian could contain himself for only fifteen seconds before his body convulsed and he cried out. He spurted his seed in waves onto the floor, as Anjelica with a practised adroitness stepped aside.

Gian stood and his eyes darted around the room in distress.

She moved her silk-clad body up against the boy, the new man, and embraced him tightly. That her dress might get a little soiled now didn't matter.

"You are beautiful," she whispered, pressing. "You might like to have a little cry now, my Gian."

　　　　Cassini's Vision

Her breasts and nipples remained pressed to his chest, then lighter, then brushing side to side delicately, deliberately, and his body remembered the brushing of Celia against him earlier.

He did weep. The experience was too intense.

Veronica brought a sweet drink and fruit, and they rested. Anjelica washed Gian and dried him, with love. Filippo cleaned the floor.

"Now, again, make eye contact with me."

"Put on your shirt, Gian," she asked after a moment. "And we will pretend to wear our masks, like this." She held hers by its handle so that it covered her upper face.

"Now come sit on the settee with me. Let's be comfortable." She arranged Gian to lie resting against her, but with his penis within reach of her hand.

Veronica and Filippo faced each other in ritual, and undressed each other, unhurried, until all they wore was their masks. For five minutes they used only their hands to caress the other, moving their palms upon one another's naked skin. Their bodies writhed and undulated under the stroking they shared. All the while their masked faces remained engaged.

Gian and Anjelica held their masks to their faces as best they could in their lounging positions. Gian's stiffness was returning under Anjelica's attentions. With her one free hand, she alternately fondled Gian and stroked his back beneath his loose shirt.

The member of Filippo had grown a little, but it still hung straight down. But it was the body of Veronica that was a surprise to Gian. As before, his knowledge of naked bodies came from observing statues and paintings at the museum galleries. There the women's bodies showed nothing but smooth skin between their legs, where men sported hair and more. But in the flesh, Veronica's sexual areas were as hairy as his own.

"Gian," whispered Anjelica, "this is real people. This is true people. After the games, the pretences, the politics. Real people are each different, and each the same. This is their life. This is their love."

He said nothing.

Veronica and Filippo lay down upon the low bed and continued the caresses. Their hands moved across their bodies, back, neck, breasts, legs—sometimes lingering, seductive. Veronica raised her knees and welcomed Filippo, and there they stayed for several minutes.

Time passed. Each was moaning—soft at first, and then urgent, breathing heavily, until they collapsed noisily.

"The roar of the beast," Anjelica whispered.

Anjelica slipped out of her silk dress. Gian saw that she too had a profusion of silky hair, red, between her legs. "You can feel it," she invited. "Please. It's my private brush."

This was foreign and frightening territory.

"His sperm inside her can make her pregnant," Anjelica said. "The way you saw, they can avoid a baby that she doesn't want just now."

On the bed, Veronica and Filippo repositioned.

"Watch," Anjelica said softly.

After a little while, Veronica was sighing and moaning. The action and the pleasure built until she finally tensed her whole body, and screamed long and shrill.

"The roar of the beast again." Anjelica wore a broad grin. Gian was awakened and quite ready.

Veronica and Filippo rested and lay close together for a long time caressing each other with a slow tenderness, each breathing the other's breath. Then they rose, stood, and, saying nothing, faced the two reclining observers.

"You can put down your mask now, Gian," said Anjelica. Veronica and Filippo removed theirs, and Gian now recognised Filippo. He was the gondolier sent this morning to fetch them from their lodgings.

Anjelica took Gian's hand. "Now it's our turn." She led him towards the bed.

The two performers straightened out their dishevelled bed to leave it inviting, and then moved to the vacated settee. They had finished their act, and they lay down naked, curled up together, to watch.

Gian was fired with embarrassment, but followed Anjelica onto the soft bed, the stage for the next drama.

For the following two hours, Mme Anjelica, courtesan irregular, introduced Gian into the ways of a man loving a woman, an education far beyond the frolics and charades of the usual Venetian establishments of entertainment.

—

With Bernardo, they took a house gondola, and proceeded northeast to the Arsenal. Bernardo was pleased to escort them, took it as a privilege. Even Antonio had not been into the Arsenal before.

"Where did the builders get so much stone for all this?" asked Gian.

Yesterday, Antonio looked him once in the eye, but otherwise Gian and Antonio had not spoken of the tryst with Mme Anjelica.

"Let's ask the first question first," replied Bernardo. "Where did this much wood come from?"

"Wood?"

"These buildings are not quite what they appear. All the foundations are wood. Venetian forests on the mainland, and imports from Montenegro and Croatia, made the long stakes driven deep into the sandy ground of the hundred islands, down, down to the clay. Thousands of stakes were sunk close together to make solid support. Wooden platforms then went onto the stakes, and the buildings of stone that you see were constructed on top of that. The water preserved the wood so that it hardens like stone anyway."

"I never could have guessed." The question of the stone was left.

The Arsenal area was fully walled in stone like a massive fortified castle complex, complete with watchtowers. At the gateway stood four Greek lions in marble, and a statue of a saint, one Giustina, to commemorate the marvellous naval victory of Lepanto.

The men surrendered their knives for a formal signing in.

"Sixteen thousand workers report in here every day," said Bernardo. "They are paid each week, served weak wine with their lunch, and are expected to do their job with fine strength and skill."

"Look from here," he said, sweeping his hand. "Those many and vast multi-storey halls and penthouses: that's what we're about to see."

First inside the gate was a museum with models of every ship and galley, and a multitude of weapons, mementos and spoils of war.

One hall was a storehouse only for oars. One stored huge nails and fixings for ship construction and repair. A massive sail loft was for cutting and curing and stitching of new galley sails.

"And this gallery has only women workers to repair the worn sails," said Bernardo.

Saltpetre for gunpowder filled another hall. A hall was devoted to cannon casting and another to scales just to weigh those cannons. Small arms and old crossbows for handfighting filled five mighty chambers, one chamber used for developing and testing only new firearms. Some areas boiled pitch, some made thick ropes, more stored cables and chains. All shapes of woodwork and ironwork for galley construction, including masts and anchors, were stored in huge numbers. Many wooden parts were from rare and special wood, some brought from afar, but most grown to order at guarded forest plantations back on Veneto's mainland territory.

All these huge halls sat around an immense square inland sea lake.

"Look out here." Perhaps fifty galleys today were sitting along the lake borders, aside the provisioning halls.

All the supply and storing galleries, and the huge lake, and other canals and offices all lay within the secretive Arsenal. The single fortified sea entrance was to the north.

"The galleys move along from store to store," explained Bernardo. "At peak construction, this Arsenal can build, and it can repair and replenish, ten galleys a day, each leaving here with full complement of sailors aboard. The Arsenal can barrack and outfit two hundred thousand seamen ready to sail.

"A hundred ships may be in the work line at any moment. Every item going onboard is built, quality-checked and counted. The galleys sail out identical to each other. This is the world's most efficient and productive construction site. Why do you think Venice has been master of the sea trade for so many centuries? We trade in goods from far away. To protect that trade, we fight war, war with the Turks, war with the Ottoman, even war with your Genoa when needed, Gian. In both the trade and the war we are the experts, and we have been for a thousand years, at the centre of the world."

Bernardo was enthusiastic, proud of his Venice.

Surely, though, Venice's supremacy has been profoundly challenged during the past hundred years. The future might be less certain than the past.

"And for the future we now have the guidance of the incomparable Galilei Reference Manual with modern and detailed instructions."

"That's Signor Galileo Galilei?" checked Gian. He recalled Galileo's talks of last week. Recalled the efficiency skills and the materials knowledge. Recalled the quality thoroughness his mentor had spoken of.

Yes, "his" mentor.

"Ah yes, that report is a first-rate asset for the Arsenal. However, we were sad to hear yesterday that he died in Florence a few days ago."

A dead mentor?

—

"What's the real reason we are going to Murano?"

They were on a gondola, the two of them and two black-clad watermen, making for the island of Murano, two miles away. The rugged gondoliers were standing, rowing to a rhythm, and chanting a soft ditty.

Antonio paused before answering. He exaggerated his voice to the accent and dialect of Genoa, different from the street speech of Venice. He leaned close to Gian's ear.

"I have a delicate commission from a company in England. My Italian is correct enough to use in Venice, but to speak in English would be dangerous for this mission. An Admiral Samuel has established a glass factory in London, and he is aware that his workers cannot produce glassware with Venetian quality, or even the glass of such crystal clarity. Samuel wants me to find skilled glassblowers who might entertain working instead in England. This information is discreet, you must understand, Gian. Do not repeat what I have told you.

"Actually, I do have more legitimate business in Murano. Every few years I notarise the company documentation for the Sicilian supplier of sand which is used for Venice glassmaking. I will pay a visit to my Murano contacts for that trade while we are here."

"Is that the jar of sand near your desk at home?"

"The same. I don't know where the Murano people get their soda ash and their limestone, and their other secret

                                    Cassini's Vision

additives, but the sand trade alone helps keep food on our table, Gian.

"Here, for you, this visit is an opportunity to see the glassworks industry, the like of which exists nowhere else on Earth."

"Can they make a lens?"

"I think they blow rather than grind. But that's your job to discover." Antonio grinned at the lad.

The smoke and the smell of burning wood was becoming stronger.

About twenty furnaces lined one side of the street, all working at once. The men entered the first building and watched from a safe distance.

As Gian stood, the glassblower used his iron tube to pick up from the crucible in the furnace a lump of molten glass. He proceeded to blow through the tube so that the glass ballooned ever larger, and by rotating rapidly and moving and touching it to his table covered with copper, he produced a large well-formed cylindrical bottle. The power of human lungs to blow glass was a marvel to see.

Twice, the bottle went back to a furnace for softening. The worker then used a sharp instrument to slit the bottle down its side. He folded the two wings down, and the bottle then lay as a flat plate onto the table. It was moved to another furnace to slowly cool, and it was then polished. This was flat glass of high quality, destined to be a mirror after they applied a backing. It took in all only a few minutes.

They walked along to another building to see its furnace. The artisan here was creating drink glasses to an order for a Syrian king. Gian had never seen a design like this, tall, intricately filigreed, and with subtle colourings, mauve, pinks and pale blues. Each glass took three minutes only to blow and shape, and each was identical to the ones before. Every glass had to be watched during cooling so it did not sag or lean.

They saw no lenses.

# Celia (b. 1625)

Celia was the second of eight children to the Bellini merchant family of Genoa. Genoa was a busy and wealthy trading port, a hub, like its competitor Venice, transferring the riches of the East to the marketplaces of Europe in the West.

Celia's elder brother Carlo died at six of the black sickness, which was a heavy grief, but it only made her stronger to survive, as she adopted the presumptions usually given only to the first-born.

The Bellinis were religious people, Catholic. Little other option applied in Italy.

From her fifth year, tutors educated Celia at home, and she made a satisfactory student. From age ten she attended the convent of Santa Maria de Castello on some days. The nuns there took a few of the daughters of the well-to-do families for schooling. As the years followed, she enjoyed most the arts, painting and music, and a little poetry. Her maternal grandmother had been famous in Rome as a painter. Had Celia inherited some of this from her grandmother?

Despite her lesser interest in languages or in the commercial subjects important to Genoa life, she was still considered a reliable child with a respectable marriageable future.

Until the burning.

—

They trudged the woman into the Piazza, and the crowd parted and fell silent. A rope hung from her neck. The priest went first, looking back at his quarry. The woman's dirty smock was yellowed with ground-in sulphur, and it was blood-stained around one breast. Her hair was matted.

Twelve-year-old Celia and her convent class friends huddled together.

At the far side of the Piazza, near to the water, was the pyre-in-waiting, a wooden stake eight feet high, and fuel of straw and faggots propped around on three sides. Extra wood sat to one side to complete the encirclement once the witch was tied up.

This was the first burning for this year.

The Padre stopped in the middle of the square, and opened his scroll. "I call upon the mighty Lord to witness our task today. Here is Maria Gilletti, found in trial to be a witch, a fornicator of the evil one, a poison on Earth and a foreigner to Heaven.

Her name Maria is to be taken from her and never again spoken, for that name belongs to the purest human that Heaven knows, the glorious mother of our blessed Saviour Jesus Christ. Diabola Gilletti is your name for your remaining moments of pitiful life, and for the records of history.

"Diabola Gilletti, woman with no husband, you are found guilty of the death of an infant that was the fruit of most despicable copulations between you and the Prince of Darkness." A roar.

"You buried this baby in the village orchard in the dark of night. Your deeds may be sins of the night, but we will punish you in the full light of the Almighty's bright day. We will burn your body here on Earth, as it can have no place resurrected into Heaven."

The priest took the rope and led Diabola to the pyre. He stepped aside as a young monk stood the woman back against the stake, and tied the neck rope to the top of the pole. Another rope fixed her hands behind her around the stake. The spare straw and wood were placed to complete the circle of fuel, with the witch's shoulders and head still visible to the crowd, now growing restive.

"Father," called a voice behind Celia, so close that Celia startled. "Father, how are we sure this woman did this deed? It was my brother found the tiny body, but we didn't know how it got there."

"She is found guilty by the Pope's court," returned the priest, "Guilty, guilty, guilty."

"Guilty, guilty, guilty," chanted enough of the assembled town to carry the day.

The monk handed the burning torch to the priest. Maria closed her eyes. With a flourish for the crowd's benefit, the priest set the torch to the bottom of the straw, and the flame took slowly. "Begone, Satan," he yelled. He lit three more tufts of straw, and stood to watch.

The fire burned. The woman remained silent.

In five minutes the breathing stopped.

Maria's head had fallen forward, her hair was frizzled stubble and her face and forehead were blackened, blistered and weeping. The tunic had finished its sulphur burn and only shreds still hung on the shoulders. With a thin branch, the priest dragged away the remaining cloth fragments. Maria's shoulders and cooking breasts lay exposed to the mob.

The crowd chattered and pointed at the body. Mothers put a hand over their children's eyes as a pretence of hiding the sight. The nuns crossed themselves. Maria's left breast, charred, was still clearly disfigured, cut away.

"She wore the mark of the Devil," shouted the priest, "an abomination."

Celia went numb.

When Celia had been five, her best playmate had been Anna. They shared houses often. Anna's mother had breast-fed them both for years. And then she suckled Anna's brother while talking with the girls, and Celia recalled the purple birthmark that ran across the mother's breast, a breast of giving and maternal comfort.

Then the peste raged through old Genova. It came on the ships, they had said. Many had died horrible deaths. Everyone stayed home, afraid to spread or catch the illness. The bodies, blackened by the plague, were collected at night and taken away to be buried in unknown places.

Celia didn't see Anna again, nor Anna's brother or father. Anna's mother was left alone, and Celia did not visit anymore. But the widow could not afford her home, and Celia never knew where she went.

Many years had passed, and time had buried the grief of losing young Anna.

Those were now the memories that tumbled back. Celia stared at the charring corpse of Anna's mother Maria.

The air throughout the square was blowing with smoke, and with the aroma of a large feast-day animal being roasted for partying.

The burning logs collapsed a little, exposing the witch's hips and legs. Her blackened flesh was splitting, overcooked, and falling away from her bones. At a signal, the monk heaped more wood onto the pyre, and soon the remains were hard to see amid the furious flames. Celia could no longer hear which crackles were from the wood, and which were from the bubbling, exploding and disintegrating body.

Neither in Heaven nor on Earth.

—

Celia fumed. She raged.

The losses years ago of Anna and Carlo had hurt her, but it was the terror and the profanity of the burning of Anna's mother that she despised with all her strength. What God endorsed such evil?

There must be a God, that was clear, but the messages and judgements of these priests could not be coming from this God. That could not be true. What her parents and the people of Genoa believed, what they were being taught to believe, had to be wrong. The world of God had to be bigger than what Genoa knew, mighty in empire though Genoa was.

The schooling continued, and Celia passed all her study tests. But her spirit was rebellious, defiant. With her classmates, she practised music and dramatics, and learned to translate her rebellion into works of art that others could see. Her father grew alarmed at the often discordant meanings embedded in her plays and poems. Still a growing child's sentiments, naive sometimes, but barbed with an angry wisdom.

After two or three years, Celia learned some tact and finesse, crafting her messages to be more acceptable to her audience, but the fire within her was lit. That fire would burn until she died.

Her girlfriends stayed loyal enough, and Celia became their mouthpiece when they themselves were still too timid to be as outspoken.

Her father's house was small but quite comfortable. He had daily business with the trading fleet, and so they lived not far from the harbour. Celia would on many days ask a friend or two to wander to the wharves with her, and sit to watch the bustling activities, the arrivals and tying up, the unloading, the sailors going ashore if they were allowed.

This was the centre ground of a commerce that spanned the known world. What lay out there where these ships sailed? What people lived there? Were they happy, or rich or poor? What did they believe in, was it rules and priests and horrible unearned punishments as we accepted here? Did God deal with these people using a different plan?

How far away did those ships go? They were scraped and buffeted and barnacled, many of them, when they came home.

Untold stories are out there. Truths not known. Facts she never suspected, realities she couldn't have guessed.

Her girlfriends listened. They nodded. They loved Celia's company. But they couldn't fathom where all the dreams and passions were coming from.

Celia's dreams by night merged into and beyond the ship scenes she sat with so often. In dream, she could by magic be transported to where people looked different, different like those sailors, to where language was mysterious and musical. But sailing on the open water was not in her dreams, just being at those other places that the sea might lead to.

—

Celia and two friends sat under the shade of a tree watching from afar the preparations for a galleon to set sail. The wind was blowing from the right direction. Sailors were slipping the ropes. Yells carried in the breeze.

From further along came two youths laughing and yelling, and struggling to roll a broken cartwheel. They made a flirting call to the girls to help them, but no one moved. The boys came alongside and stopped. After an embarrassed silence, the taller one asked for some water. The day was warm and the task was taxing.

Celia stretched her arm in theatre. "How much do you want? Water stretches from here to past Sicily."

The tall one grinned. "Just a small jar of drinkable water would be a gift from a goddess."

"Gods don't come as goddess," she retorted. She did however appreciate the promotion. It showed.

Celia's friend fetched from her bag a skin with a little water and offered it to the boys.

"What is the story of this wheel?" asked Celia. It had two broken spokes and the rim had lost its iron and it was cracked.

"It came from a god. Or perhaps a goddess."

"Oh?"

"No, a net loaded with sacks was being unloaded from that ship along the bank this morning, and it all slipped and crushed a cart. The cart was wrecked. Even the other wheel was crumpled. Then we took this wheel. It has nearly survived."

"But," said Celia, "won't the owner want to salvage what he can? This wheel might repair."

"We decided he didn't want it. He died under the sacks too."

Silence.

"Well," said the girl who offered the water skin, "what are you planning with your broken one wheel?"

The tall fellow looked back to Celia.

The other boy responded. "We will just keep it. We don't know how to fix it. But it might make a good part for an artwork. Francho here makes art out in the fields. Not real art, paint and brushes art, just things arranged, coloured and joined together, to make you stop and think."

Another silence.

"I do art a different way," Francho said quietly. "We see things we had no idea were there. They weren't there. Until ..."

—

Sometimes Celia still sat by the waterfront with her girlfriends watching the harbour activity. On two occasions Francho joined them to watch and talk. Celia's mother was terrified her daughter was coming to harm and scandal, but Celia by now was no longer responsive to parental guidance.

True, a little flirting happened all around, but both Francho and Celia learned to hide that spark they started with. Francho and Celia was a transaction to be conducted separately and with discretion and discreetness.

Francho took her one afternoon to a quiet gully where he had positioned his ill-gotten cartwheel between two trees, hinged in the manner of a dysfunctional gate.

"What does it mean?"

"What does it mean for you? My meaning may be different."

"I want to know what is beyond such a strange gate."

"That I can't tell you."

Celia swung the gate open and stepped through. She returned. "I can't see that anything was there."

"Keep looking. Always a reality is there you didn't know about."

Once more she stepped through. Francho leaned through his gate and kissed her, but only briefly.

Celia jumped back, reached and slammed the gate, and ran around from behind it. She hurried home unable to understand her own confusion.

Next week Francho and Celia walked out again to the art gate. They left it unopened, and sat on the ground for an hour discussing what mysteries might lie beyond. Fantasies. Lost family that they never knew. Far places never yet seen. Secret dream scenes from the deep of night. Stretching distances past imagining. Sailing always boldly. Across seas. Beyond skies.

They barely touched.

Several times during the following month, they met at the art gate. They came no closer than touching hands, but increasingly Celia's emotions were torrid and tangled.

Late one afternoon she hurried to her rendezvous place, and was alerted first to the voices of two boys arguing in the ravine. She crept closer to hear what was said.

"Pervert. A disgrace. Every week I see you go out here, and now all I find is a collection of strange objects in the forest. Are you a witch?"

"Bruno, I'm not. I just like to make unusual images here to explain my world."

"Francho, I think you are a witch. Witches are evil."

As Celia watched in horror, Bruno pulled out a knife. She sprang up and raced forward to intervene, but already Francho had been stabbed in the heart and had fallen.

"Franchoooo," she cried.

She tried to lift his body—but she was too late. Blood was spreading, and Francho's eyes stayed unseeing.

The killer stared at his deed, stunned at Celia's arrival.

Before Bruno could respond further, Celia snatched the knife from his hand.

"You madman. What have you done?"

"He had to die. He was a witch. And he loves other strange boy witches. Together they make this God-hating scenery."

"Francho was not any witch. He was a gentle man who loved and thought and created beauty." She paused an instant. "He was, he was ..." Again she hesitated. "He was my boyfriend." She waved the knife at Bruno.

"Stop. Francho was evil," and Bruno lunged for the knife. She sidestepped.

Celia's heart was raging. She was not arguing more. As Bruno spun, she plunged the blade into the boy's chest, and he staggered and fell.

Hurriedly, Celia checked the scene of her disaster. She found that Bruno was carrying a second knife in his clothing. The second one she bloodied, and she left both knives near the bodies.

She headed for home, but decided instead to go by the harbour where she could wash her hands. Sitting on the wall and staring at the salty undrinkable water, Celia contemplated what might lie beyond Sicily, beyond Malta, far beyond where anyone had ever been daring or able to look.

She kept her silence. Enquiries into the forest deaths of two of the town's youths did not involve her. That pain she stored in her heart, alongside some others.

—

"A clock. Any clock," she said. "My parents have bought a clock, and I want to know why it works. Gian, you understand machines better than other boys. Come out and tell me about clocks. It's Christmas, and I hate this potato, and it's noisy in here. Come on. No one will notice."

A nude statue in the current high fashion stood at a fountain in Antonio's garden. "Don't mind my Uncle's sculpture," Gian apologised.

She laughed. "It's art, silly. You don't be sorry about art. It's to help us to understand."

"Oh."

She walked to the statue and flicked one stone nipple with her finger, and watched his alarm.

"Firstly, it's only a piece of marble. Secondly, it's there to change our soul somehow, change what we know."

"Perhaps it's like time," she continued. "How do we know what that is? The clock seems to count bits of time. But what is that time?"

Cassini was looking confused. What was in his head? Did he think she was dangerous? Did he think the question was nonsense? His face was blushing. But he was still watching her and listening, waiting.

"Gian, I'm teasing you. We all know what time is. I think we do. But I want to figure out how my parents' clock is so precise in counting time. You're smart. Your family knows that. You pull things apart and study them. You know how they work. Explain it to me. My friends say our clock has a spirit. I think you know better."

"I do have a clock that I haven't finished examining yet," he said. "In a week I will check your clock as well."

She calculated they had both won.

"Then we can consider further what this time is," she said. She touched his shoulder. This one she would not lose.

—

Her invitation came from cousin Antonio. Merely a "casual afternoon visit with refreshment". His son Giovanni had asked that she visit to inspect a clock he had acquired and was rebuilding. He believed the Signorina may be interested. Would she deign to accept?

Celia knew that Gian was not Antonio's son, but she let that pass. Yes, thank you, Celia accepts with respect, she had her parents send back.

Her father escorted her to the Crovese household, and remained with Antonio for the duration of the appointed visit.

"How awkward is this?" she remarked. "Is this the only way to take a look at a clock?"

"Celia, my Uncle understands this protocol," he said. "Families need to believe they are protecting their children."

"Protecting you from me?"

"Protecting you from me, more likely."

"Gian, in my short life thus far I have learned that my best protection comes when I provide for myself. Where's this wretched clock?"

A kitchen servant knocked and entered with tea and a plate of small cakes, smelling fresh-baked.

The clock stood on a table to one side, covered with a cloth. Gian removed the cover. "Here."

"You have it working now?"

It was smaller than she expected. Her mother's clock hung on her wall, and it was rather larger and more ornate than this older clock.

"Yes, it works." He reached behind the clock and held out for her a scrap of coiled thread. "This is what was broken."

"You may need to impress me more than that," she laughed.

They drank their tea. She looked at the clock, pensive.

Gian's clock was a box shape, a mere palm-width high, and it had its clock face on top. It had a single hand for showing the time, which was indicated with old Roman numerals for the hours, and quarter-hour marks between the hours.

"Why do you need a clock?"

"For astrological readings, I need to know the time you were born, and the precise positioning of the stars and planets at that birth time. With a clock, we can observe and record planet transitions more accurately."

"You must read my stars one day. But now, can you show me what this clock does? And then I want to know how it works."

"Of course." Into the side of the clock he placed a tubular key with a winding knob on it. He wound the knob a little, and it made a clicking sound.

"Put your ear to the clock, like this."

She did so. "It is making a steady tick sound. Ours does the same, though."

"It's counting time. If you wait and watch, you can see the hand moving, ever so slowly."

"But it is too slow. My mother's clock has two hands, and only the one that tells us the hours is slow like this."

"Now, in a few moments it will be right on the hour three. A bell should ring."

"My mother's doesn't make any noise like that."

They waited.

As expected, the ring of three bells marked the hour.

"And that's it. Every day I wind the curled metal spring. Some days at midday by the sundial outside I alter this timing hand a little to agree. It does lose its accuracy a little."

"It's quite old. It's tarnished."

"Of course it's old. It wasn't used anymore."

"Where did you get it? Where did it come from?"

"I had it open to fix it, and inside it was marked Nuremberg."

He'd answered only half the question.

"My parents said ours is from Prague. What I want to know is, how does it work?"

"Look at this conical part inside, with the gut string wound around it." The clock had a glass window on its front wall, and the mechanical parts were easy to see.

"That's to compensate for the spring unwinding for twenty-four hours and losing its strength. That lower spring strength would make the clock go slower later in the day, not holding a constant ticking speed."

"No, that's all boring. How does it really work? My girlfriend says that a spirit, a resident mini-god, is in control, handing out time at a steady speed."

"What do you think?"

"I don't know. Perhaps time just flows through at a regular rate, and the clock has a part that can catch the flow as it passes, and it connects that constant speed to the hands."

"Explain more."

"Sure. I go sometimes to watch the old mill outside town. The creek water flows past at a constant speed. The paddle wheel is in that water, and the paddles latch onto the water speed. That speed gets connected to the millstone which continues at its same speed all the time. Except the stone is slower in dry weather, though. The miller has let me watch a few times ..."

Celia looked up at Gian.

"Possibly paddles in the clock catch the time flowing past in the same way?" I'm begging, she thought.

Gian was silent for a while. He was about to let her down gently? Please?

"Gian, when I examine anything closely, I come to see that I hadn't ever understood it correctly at all. My friends didn't believe things I assumed they did. Ships' barnacles don't grow only in faraway places, they grow a little in any water, and here in harbour. I learn that things the virtuous Fathers tell us in Church cannot be true after all.

"Half-knowing things, not asking more questions, means not caring for the real truth. I want all my life to keep looking, keep asking questions. And then, asking again."

Oh, dear. That might lose this man right now.

"How does this clock work?" she asked, barely audible.

"I can tell you how it works." He smiled.

"Did you ever as a child play at rocking in the woods or outside your house? You and a playmate sitting at the ends of a plank of wood or a clean straight branch? And the centre of the plank was balanced on a log, so that you both could bounce up and down? I'm going to put you inside our clock."

He had a tool to remove the glass window at the front and a rear brass panel. Now it was easy to see the parts inside. The clock was still ticking.

A brass bar in the rear was rocking, and that was the source of the tick. It was fixed with a metal pin at its centre, and it was oscillating up and down.

"Your description is close. This tiny rocking beam is adjusted so that it always rocks at the correct speed. The ticks stay at that same speed all day and night. We could say that the rocker catches the same little second of time on each tick. Like your paddle wheel takes the same number of seconds between each turn."

"It's that simple?"

"Yes."

"It isn't exactly what I had been thinking—but it does make sense to me."

No.

But ...

Gian showed how for every tick, the rocker allowed the big gear wheel to move one small position in its circle, and then the hour hand moved in step with that, to a fixed timing.

"Do we look another time at your parents' new clock?"

"Ours has no window to see what is inside. But I have discovered what I need on clocks now. I think I'm a little sad that my girlfriend's godlet was not in there."

"However," she continued, "I would like that you could still visit our house. It's not a spacious house, because it's near the old harbourfront, but it does have some spare space. In the front room by our door, my parents allowed me to set up a studio. I paint there and twice I have had a modest exhibition. Last week I sold a canvas, my first."

"That's amazing. Yes, I'll visit."

"And I have a favour to ask. I have started to practise miniature marble sculptings, and a corner of my room has dust and stone chips that don't belong in a painting studio. My few little sculptures are not very good. The paintings I enjoy, and I feel in some control, but on the small marble work I am struggling. Would you come and offer some opinions."

"I know nothing of painting, or of sculpting, but I guess I can give you my amateur opinions."

"Thank you. Please come."

"But tell me, what are your paintings about? Floral, or landscapes? Portraits, maybe? Portraits would be difficult."

"They are things I see. Sometimes ordinary things. But always there is something else trying to be in my art, something more than what is obviously there."

"How do I understand that?"

"I don't know, Gian. I want someone else, someone I can trust, to view them with me."

Someone with me.

—


Celia was envious. Gian was out of town with his Uncle for the month.

Gone to Venice.

Venice had that artistic reputation, that wild independent spirit that Celia wanted to live. Venice promised the unexpected.

She waited.

This morning, her canvas beckoned. As in a trance, she organised her paints, checked the brushes. It started as a circle that had no reasons, no meanings, and it morphed into a circular gateway among many trees. She recognised it in her stupor, but did not control it. The foreground became grasses and weeds, a fallen log. Clear. Beyond the circle was grey, nothing that made sense or artistic fabric. The grey stayed piteously empty, asking, seeking. In her spell nothing placed itself there in that grey.

Her hand was shaking, wanting to create.

Celia sat down and looked up at her work, unfinished, unfinishable, and she cried. She felt small.

The canvas stayed pinned to her easel until next day, and then she took the uncompletable and cut it to shreds. This she had never done before.

About the lad Bruno she made discreet enquiries: he had been the favourite altar boy of the priest on the other side of town. Another story again must be hidden there, but to reseal her silence she left the matter.

She continued waiting for Gian's return. She wanted that mind in her life.

—

He knelt on her floor in the dark corner of the studio room, sweeping out each tiny fragment and the white stone dust.

"This stone has found its way into every crevice and under every shelf," he complained. "It's been here for months."

"I'm an artist," she pleaded. Where would being coy take her?

"No, that's not a real excuse."

It took her nowhere.

"Gian, I'm frustrated with the little sculptures. I'm not succeeding. Everything I try becomes awkward and has no style."

"Show me how you use your hammer and the tools."

One piece, barely started, was nearby, and she placed it on her low and solid bench. "It should be a sitting girl, and the first larger pieces to remove are here, and here." They were marked.

She held her hammer and struck one timid blow. A chip flew across the room.

She looked at where the stone had flown.

"I'm worried about the paintings." She turned to him.

"It's not your medium, is it?"

She closed her eyes and shook her head. "No. But I want it to be."

"No, you don't. Did you study marble sculpting at school?"

She hadn't. Poetry she loved. Acting she had tried, and that was promising too. The painting was her real passion, and her success, where she was comfortable with herself.

She left the room and in a moment returned with two earlier abandoned attempts in marble. Saying nothing, Gian turned them over in his hands, looking.

In sculpting she had had no guidance, no training, no mentor. It was her private ambition to learn for herself, to add it to her repertoire.

"But I can't do it, Gian."

"And that's the truth?"

"Yes, it is, but I haven't known how to admit, accept it."

"And it is you who tells me that we must seek and know the truth, even the truth we were not expecting."

Together they cleaned up the room, returning it to the modest studio it once was. The sculpting items they packed into a box, perchance one day Celia felt brave to start again.

From then on, he visited the studio frequently. The adventures in Venice (some of them) he told her several times, and she envied him again. She persuaded him to sketch the gondolas, and the famed Rialto Bridge, from his memory. His recall was clear, but his sketching skills were mediocre. The glass artists and their colourful ornaments she wanted to hear about again and again.

The discussions with Sig. Galilei she heard played out many times. Each telling was subtly a different story, as Cassini processed for himself all the meanings of his meeting with Galilei. "Which version is the true one?" she teased.

"They are all the real story. The real story of Signor Galilei was bigger than any time I try to tell it. Always I hear him at the end offering the same message as you do: there's a truth always beyond what you imagine. Keep searching."

—

On some days, Gian brought Galilei's old pendulum manuscript to her studio, along with the old German clock. As she painted, he pored over the treatise.

He learned when Celia was painting not to chatter and disrupt. Her painting was her own journey, and she neither spoke nor stopped. She said she was "communing".

So he studied Galilei's attempts to harness the regular rhythm of the pendulum to be the timekeeper in a better clock. And he sketched ways he might make his own practical design of an escapement.

"Oh, the mathematics," he complained once. "It was important at school, and I downplayed it."

When Celia had done with her painting, she emerged from her reverie and became again the woman he knew. The Celia he liked. The Celia he loved spending time with. It made her glow.

One morning, Celia brought to see him her artist girlfriend Cristina. Cristina wanted her horoscope read, because she was considering whether to continue the study that her fortunate parents could still afford, or to prepare to enter a nunnery. She was not seeking a convent as any solution to poverty, not being urged by her parents, but rather she genuinely was impressed with the holy and devoted life of the nun.

Gian asked about her birth. What date and where, and what minute of the day or night? Were there any other details of her birth that she could provide?

Cristina went home to ask more questions in her family, as she had never thought about such detail. Two mornings later she returned.

"Here in Genoa, in the same house I now live in," she reported. "Father says it was an hour or two before sunrise. He recalls it well."

Gian consulted his records of planet trajectories and times, the ephemeris, and drew up Cristina's birth chart. But a chart with its houses and signs means nothing without the interpretation, and interpretation of charts was a study he had spent long hours on.

When you were born, in which sign and house did each planet lie? Each sign and planet, each house has a meaning or an influence, and those need to be seen as a connected whole. How these influences take expression through your life can be intuited by studying the relationships of their positions on your chart.

As we live our life, the cycles of our life on Earth map with the cycles of the planets around the Earth, and another chart made for today, taken alongside your birth chart, can give a strong prediction of what is happening in your life now.

By now, Cristina had grown restless.

Gian sat with the two girls, and he interpreted the chart's meaning for Cristina's character. When Cristina felt comfortable with that, then he laid out what predictions or possibilities he saw ahead for her.

When he stopped his reading, Cristina sat in silence for a long while.

Then, "I know now. My life belongs to God. Thank you, Gian."

—

In four months, Gian had collected two additional old clocks, and his research intensified.

In the same four months, Celia had assembled a useful collection of finished works. Together they arranged to hang her art to best effect in the little studio, and they made notices about the town inviting all to visit.

"Did you know your Uncle visited here once?"

"No. He never said."

"I saw him. It was a poetry day."

—

The seaport life, the activity on the wharves had been a love of Celia for years. She taught her Gian how to sit under the same trees, watching the same ships coming, going and unloading and refitting. Sniffing the salty air. Seeing the sailors working or going off to town. Listening to the rowdy dock workers. Checking if they knew which merchants were with effective diligence watching their goods go aboard or come off. Seeing noisy carts taking stuffs between here and the warehouses some streets back.

Often they took a little food, to more enjoy the spectacle. "What's out there, Gian?"

It was under these old and humble trees, near the harbourfront of the port of Genoa, hub of a vast Italian trade empire, that Giovanni Cassini, talented rescued orphan, was introduced to the poetry and magic of Celia Bellini, artist and wily, wayward child of a successful shipping merchant.

# Panzano

Signora Celia Bellini Cassini, now swollen with her first child, sat heavily onto a wooden stool by the bench of her new kitchen. She had worried their newly constructed professor's residence would have the traditional hard earth and replaceable straw that she was familiar with from her youth, from the days before her father could afford his new harbourside house.

This Cassini house, however, completed only last week, and smelling so new, had modern tiled floors that were so much easier and cleaner than the old floors she remembered. She had no house servants yet, and housework had not been part of her life.

Gian and Celia had married last year to much family and town pomp, and they had lived for the while with Antonio's family. The art studio stayed at the harbourfront Bellini house, and most days Celia walked there and painted. For both Genoa families the arrangement served well, as they continued to see their children in their lives.

It was four months ago that the Marquis Cornelio Malvasia had visited Antonio and Celia's young husband Giovanni. The Senator was building a grand project at Panzano near Bologna, a new telescope observatory and study centre.

The Marquis was a keen adherent, an entrepreneur, of astrology, and of astrology's intimate connection to close observations and timing of heavenly bodies. He had also, since the Crovese visit to his house three years ago, kept himself apprised from afar of the skills and energy of the young Cassini he had met.

Malvasia then offered to her Gian, Giovanni Cassini of Genoa, with a young but respected reputation both in astrology and in technical observation and recording, the inaugural professorship of his Panzano Astronomical Observatory.

—

Malvasia was building a full walled-in villa complex at Panzano, including an astronomy observation tower, accommodation for the professor and family, further accommodations, servant quarters, client consultation rooms, lecture theatres, and other small hamlet structures. Most was still being completed, and only the tower and the professor's residence were usable so far.

The new Observatory itself was a square tower with a viewing platform on its top. The tower was built in fine brick. Thick from the ground up, the Observatory walls would ensure the deck would be a solid base for telescopes, immune to wind sway or ground vibration.

Not looking a lot different, Cassini thought, from a lookout tower on a castle, or on an old monastery. Probably stronger.

Under the deck was a working room for writing, resting, or escaping the weather when not viewing. At ground level was a store area. The deck had no roof, and any minor equipment there would have to be moved inside in inclement weather, and telescopes and major items would need covering and tying down. The deck edges were fenced in brick, and a thick cloth rooftop could be fastened over it all from fence to fence in bad conditions.

Cassini set about preparing the observation area for its mission. The builders and carpenters had gone from the tower when he arrived from Genoa, and all was empty apart from stray litter. On that first morning, he cleaned up, and then he stood his makeshift personal telescope, made crudely using Galileo's lenses and a long tube, into centre place.

He fetched Celia to see.

However, the Marquis arrived first. The light telescope had blown over. "Ready for work, I see? And good morning, Signora."

"No," Cassini said, with a grin. "Not today."

"I have one Campani telescope from Rome that arrived here a few days ago. Fine instrument. The latest design. This afternoon I'll send two men here, and we can haul it up and mount it where you decide. Think about how you would position a writing or sketching table, and a little weatherproof storage for what's always needed up here. You may be working here a great deal of the night, remember. What about water jugs?

"And also, young Signor Professor, should we install a horoscope charting table in the room under us?"

"No, that's not a smart idea, Signor Marquis, if I may say. The tower is for astronomical observations and recording. Making a chart is a different function altogether, although it uses planet timings.

"Could we not use one of the small rooms near to your consultation parlour? It should be more salubrious and elegant for your client, an entertaining space even, near the front or centre of the Villa. You can say to your client, come here into the charting studio. Here is where we start your horoscope, incorporating the latest of our planetary readings."

The Villa was not yet inhabited.

"You are right, yes. I was not thinking this out fully," said Malvasia.

"I'll think of the room under us as an astronomical study. Somewhere where you or I can work when not looking through eyepieces. We will have visitors here also, but these visits will more directly be on the science of the astronomy."

—

One of the Villa rooms nearer to the front entrance than the astronomy tower was to be a lecture and presentation room for scientific audiences. Cassini was the appointed professor, and therefore was the principal astronomy teacher. Today they were working with the carpenters and labourers finishing the woodwork and the student benches. The design owed some credit to the Bologna Theatre they both had visited a few years earlier, but smaller and without the lavish adornment of gods and muses.

Cassini was registering quite how fanatical the Marquis was about his astrology. Malvasia was a wealthy citizen, wealth built not only from his family tradition, but also from his own wits. In astrology he could intuit, as true entrepreneurs ever had done, how shrewd advice offered to the confused and hesitating, especially the well-to-do confused and hesitating, was a mine that held vast treasures for the miner.

The astrology business, making predictions and offering best-risk advice, was now becoming very competitive. Across Europe, elite astrology services to the regal, the noble, the trade captains, and to the Cardinals too, were being measured and contrasted by the authority and accuracy of the star and planet timings on which the horoscopes were cast. Planetary observations, however, were the task of astronomy.

"It was the fault of this new toy, this invention called telescope, Giovanni."

Which is why he needs an astronomy professor in his institute, Cassini reminded himself. Malvasia was speaking openly. Quite pragmatic. He must trust me, must know we have to work together.

"While the Venetian nobles were excited to use their telescope for maritime surveillance, some like that crazy Galilei had pointed it upwards to study the planets, and were too willing to tell what they found."

Cassini struggled to keep his face straight, but thankfully Malvasia was not looking.

"The Pope's Inquisition had Galilei's arrogance thrown in their face, and therefore they quashed him."

"Your job here," he said, "is to use our telescope to peer once more at the planets."

"And to have the Inquisition burn us to death?"

"Not at all. We are not looking for any heretical breakthrough, any awkward items out there, or new explanations on how things move. Let's not be fools. Let's not be martyrs over issues the Pope has decreed upon. If we see things that are not acceptable, then we practise our holy faith to submit to God's unfathomable mystery."

"Marquis, do you believe that?"

No answer.

A moment later, Malvasia continued.

"Your job, our job, is to observe and to record with ever-increasing detail and precision the positions of all the astrological bodies, minute by minute, with the best clocks and the best telescopes. We, you and me, become the undisputed owners and masters of our truth, the most complete compendium of the epherimides that underpin the astrology readings. I understand the business of astrology. You and I will record the details of the heavens as none have before."

Gian sought clarification on what "You and I will record the details" might mean.

Most weeks, Senator the Marquis Malvasia of Bologna would spend one day and evening at the Villa. He could entertain in his salon clients seeking readings, and impress them with a tour of the modern and efficient Observatory. On occasions, he would use the lecture room for learned astrology presentations to select clients. On cloudless evenings he might stay into the dark, and contribute some planet recordings with Cassini.

The Villa/Observatory was the Marquis's property, and he would fund whatever facilities it might need, including telescopes.

Professor Cassini was resident manager of the Villa property. He received a moderate stipend for a comfortable life a little outside the Bologna town, sufficient to support a family and some staff. He would conduct open-ended astronomical research and recordings, but especially as could assist the astrological charting. At intervals, he would give public astronomy lectures revealing the latest heavenly findings, and enhancing the Observatory's scientific reputation.

Gian arrived home late; that he would be away late into the nights would be a part of their married life from now on.

He walked in from the dark, carrying his copper lantern, with its squat tallow candle burning inside. Extinguishing that lantern, he placed it with the three others inside his doorway.

Their baby was due soon. Celia had arranged that a visiting local wet-nurse, a balia, would share her coming burden.

Celia sat with Gian as he ate a supper she had put together for him.

Two reed rushlights were burning, clipped in their handmade metal holders at a 45-degree angle to burn well, and setting a comforting light across the dining bench. Celia had found cheap rushlights sold in bundles at the small Panzano market.

Anna's mother Maria, she remembered, used long ago make her own rushlights from reeds whittled to be little more than their pith, and from soaking those then in mutton tallow.

The rushlights were fragile, and Celia had broken several in her first lightings.

"Explain to me again. What did the Marquis say?"

"He wants the constellations and planets observed and recorded in ever more detail. His reputation as an astrologer is to be built on that detail."

"This far, that's excellent. He rates you the best available astronomer. Go over the next part of what he wants."

"He's wary of the Inquisition. Don't invite trouble. Stick to the ephemeris."

"Don't believe what you might see? Gian, you promised me." She did not yell, did not raise her voice. She just looked at him. "Solemnly promised."

He had.

"Gian, what's our future?"

"Professor of Astronomy is a fantastic start in our life!"

"Yes, it is. And then?"

"Then?"

"We are away from the city. I need to adapt to this. I'm an artist. Artists need friends who are artists. You are an astronomer. Or do I still label you an astrologer?"

"First, stop there. We have this job because I have studied and I understand astrology, and because I make a good observer, especially with the telescope. The telescope ties in with astrology. The more I work with the Marquis and the more I work with my telescope, the less I respect the divinations and the more I believe facts I can observe and verify."

"I don't call you an astrologer then?"

"No."

"Now we have two problems."

"No, no, no. I can play my role as astronomer well and at the same time provide the Marquis with what he needs. In private I can downplay the astrology."

"And your studies, Gian? You had planned more."



Cassini's Vision

"Mathematics I want to study more. Modern astronomy needs mathematical skills, and rather more than I have. I had thought I might walk into Bologna once each week. To suit my times, I may have to pay for private classes."

"Gian, I'm scared."

He looked on his wife, flushed, fertile, vulnerable. He loved her ever more.

—

Celia enquired of the Marquis whether she might use a room in the Villa to be a studio. She had identified a room that thus far was unused.

The Marquis had other plans, he said.

She had a next option: a smaller room in the professor's accommodation that she and Gian now made ready. The light into the new studio was not optimal, but she promised to make do with that.

If they had more babies, then they would need to consider how to share out the space available.

"I can work here, it will be sufficient. I can accept that."

"But you are bothered, I can tell."

"I can accept working here, I said that."

A minute passed.

"It's the answer from Malvasia. It hurt me."

Another pause.

"I can believe he may have a use in his mind for that spare room. And that too I could accept. It was the attitude I felt he showed me. I was simply rejected. I wasn't important."

Giovanni didn't know how to appease her just now.

The Marquis had employed him, and was not sparing in funding and implementing that. But he was an aggressive and successful Italian man of business and a busy politician. There may be times when they had to accept that what was available was the wisest choice, and not pine for what was not there on offer.

—

"What skills do you bring that might be useful for the position I am offering?"

"I would understand," started Borso, "that you need a fit healthy young person who is practical, able to measure and construct and even design mechanical objects. Able to repair working instruments when necessary. Capable of being assigned a task and then being independent and resourceful to do that job. Someone you could trust."

"That's a reasonable summary," replied Giovanni. "We have two telescopes, mechanical drawing tables, water tanks, accurate clocks, for example, and models of the stars and planets around Earth. I would require you to maintain those and more, clean them and keep them in top condition, and sometimes fabricate others. I would also require you to be my assistant on any other tasks I need to do as a researcher, and at times as a teacher."

Borso nodded.

"When I travelled, I would need you to be my travel assistant. Might that be any problem?"

Borso stifled a laugh. "Professor Cassini, travel is no problem. I have travelled for two years past Constantinople, by ship and on land."

"You can read?"

"In most Italian dialects, and French and Farsi."

Farsi? What was Farsi?

"Very well. You were also asked to bring evidence of mechanical skill."

"I have that." He reached into his satchel, and placed on the bench an old ship's compass. The compass itself, no surrounding gimbals for levelling.

"I'm impressed. Continue."

"I repaired this once on board ship, but the second time it was faulty, I found the broken point bearing ... here ..."

He unclipped its glass cover, ran his finger around the weather seal tenderly, familiarly, touched the cardinal points on its multi-point rose, and then exposed the pivot bearing. Its point was corroded.

"We had nothing with us at sea to fix that properly, and we put into service the emergency spare compass, which was a lot newer."

"Did you then steal this?"

"No, I won it in a fair wager."

Gian lifted from behind his desk a complex spherical brass device. "What do you think this is? What's it for?"

"That is a version of astrolabe. It measures the altitude above horizon of stars or planets. May I feel it?"

Gian had seen enough of the skills Borso brought with him. There was one more question. Or was it a question to himself? He would put it a different way.

"Borso, if we work together, I would want you to report to me truthfully whatever we may see out there. If it's crazy, still tell me. On what you know, if it makes no sense, still tell me. When I don't understand or you think I don't, tell me again."

Borso acknowledged, but Cassini had no confidence he understood the request.

The man stood tall, hair curly, muscles firm, eyes clear.

Borso the next day entered Cassini's employ.

It was days later before Borso admitted the Constantinople connection. "I was taken as slave for two years, sorry."

He stayed on.

—

During the first year at Panzano, Gian and Celia Cassini developed a custom of having guests to dinner on many Friday evenings. They reserved Friday as family dinner time in any case, guests or no. Borso, who lived adjoining the professor residence, had been Friday guest several times, and soon he became a regular. The core group now was Gian and Celia, their baby Lucia, usually Borso, and even the new cook/servant girl Bianca, who was in and out of the dining room while also providing the meal.

The informality of what constituted "family" surprised some guests, but the Cassinis lived to their own rules.

Any guest on a Friday was explicitly invited to a social occasion, not work. When Cassini wanted a more formal or business dinner meeting, he held that on a different day.

The cleric Battista Riccioli was tonight's Friday guest. Gian knew this man. This was the telescope tutor of his Abbey days.

Malvasia also knew Riccioli well. Both lived in Bologna, not two miles away.

Father Battista was famous now in telescopes and astronomy, and he had himself used that early Galilei telescope. Battista was mapping the Moon, and he now owned a better instrument from the Roman maker Divini. Malvasia's was by the other Roman telescope fabricator Campani, and Malvasia and Battista vied and bragged about whose was the better. Battista improved and calibrated his own, but Malvasia would have his young professor Cassini work on the Campani one at Panzano.

And so, early in the Cassini life at Panzano, Battista Riccioli and Giovanni Cassini were re-introduced. Two experts with a common passion. An instant rapport, but with an element of mentor and disciple.

Tonight, Battista was enjoying the Cassini food and wine. Bianca had served up a roasted leg of mutton.

To a hungry family, nothing smells so urgent as a roast mutton. Bianca had brought in the carved meat on one dish. Being both cook and serving maid in this household, she had learned to make a theatrical ceremony of serving all from a standing position at one end of the table. A place at table was set for her to sit with them, but she most of the time was up organising. Battista, like a few guests before him, accommodated to the Cassini way.

"What's the red sauce, Bianca?"

     

"A carrot and quince sauce, Signor. Cooked and cooled and strained. Pope's food, Signor. I do good Pope's food."

Battista laughed.

As always, work discussions were not allowed. As always, that rule got a little bent at times. Tonight they persuaded Battista to recall his memories of Galileo Galilei.

"Oh, he was a clever man, Galilei, but I thought I had found him out."

"Found him wrong?"

"I was sure I had. More than ten years ago, he wrote an extensive treatise covering many of his discoveries. Two things caught my attention. One discovery was a problem and another was wrong, I decided.

"He contradicted Aristotle's teaching that has stood unchallenged for two thousand years. Aristotle said heavier objects fall faster. It's obvious that they should, no? Galilei now claimed that, if we excepted light fluffy things like a feather which can catch in the wind, then lighter objects like a small rock and heavier ones like a cannonball will fall at the same speed.

"He also asserted that for each successive second of falling, the distance any object falls is firstly one length of fifteen Roman feet, then three times that, then five times, seven, nine and so on. Always odd numbers."

Battista shook his head.

"I'm a careful man, and this all sounded rash, wrong. Galilei didn't describe where or how he arrived at his measurements. Many of his notes on this were in any case prohibited from publication by the Vatican's Index. But I have influence."

He grinned.

"I still managed to access both his Latin and Italian versions."

"So I read him again," he said. "Had I misunderstood him? No. He was outright wrong. I set out using the Asinelli leaning tower in Bologna and a miniature pendulum to show his readings were wrong."

"And?"

"Well, I discovered he was exactly right."

"Did you hide that information?" Gian looked across to Celia. She glared back.

"Of course not. It was the truth. I took the results straight to Father Cavalieri, our Chair of Mathematics in Bologna. He's an ailing old man and confined to bed, but he was ecstatic. He had been a close colleague of Galilei. And being in that profession, he could see they were birthing a new mathematics of falling."

Discussion during the evening moved on to local politics and University scandals. Battista was a source of the sauciest tales of misdemeanour, to the merriment of all.

Bianca served up poached marasca cherries set in jelly.

"Galilei again," said Celia. "Was he a brave man also?"

"Well, yes. And no. What put him in trouble was not bravery in speaking his findings. It was his foolishness, his hubris. He gave no sensitivity to those he was refuting. The man never let anyone down with any dignity when he believed he had observed carefully, reasoned his case without error, and had come with conviction to new facts. He was a bull."

That feeble man who had set the direction in Gian's life.

"Always we should speak the facts we find. But I believe also that always we should treat the old adversary with respect.

"And with that I must bid you good night. The Moon shines bright outside, but the riding is slow. Borso, would you come help me saddle my horse please?"

                    Cassini's Vision

# Borso

Gian lifted his old astrolabe from under its wraps on his study shelf, and handed it to Borso.

"It's time you explained yourself, young Borso." Borso was in fact the same age. "What do you know about astrolabes?"

Borso took the sphere and danced around the room with it, caressed it.

The professor's eyes widened. "Bring back my treasure."

Instead, Borso spun himself along the floor until he reached the end of the room, where he placed the machine with care on a table, and he careened again back to the centre of the room.

"Borso!"

"Shhh ... I hear the flutes. I feel the dance. I revolve with the universe."

"Borso!"

Borso stopped his spinning and opened his eyes.

"What on the Lord's splendid Earth were you doing?"

"Sorry master."

"I am not your slave master. Not ever."

"My master taught me to dance. It's a Persian journey to happiness."

"Explain."

Borso paused a while.

"We danced in circles because the whole universe forever revolves about our Earth, and we signify all that turns. All men can join in the dance of the universe, and weave with the harmony and order. Our body yields to the movement of all the planets and stars, and Sun and Moon. As the body sways and our blood goes hot, our mind and our eternal soul become free from earthly bondage, free from our earthly body. We can become whole, part of the totality, the eternity and the truth of life."

"Why do I suspect you may have had help from smoking the sufi hemp?"

"No, I promise. Well, only once."

Borso crossed to the table and brought back the astrolabe. "Sorry, ma..."

"Don't."

"Sorry."

"Right. We should start again. What do you know about astrolabes? You have used one, I know. Was it for astrology measurements? "

"I have seen several types. The one we had was not spherical like this but flat, a quadrant of a circle. Once, I accompanied my master into India, and each night we used his device to take polestar readings so we could better know our location in the desert, and if we had wandered off course. When I studied how it worked, I could explain it and operate it far better than he could. Tomorrow I can show you the one I brought home from Persia. I can demonstrate it for you."

"I didn't steal it," he added.

"Could you repair mine? It was badly handled long ago, and is bent a little."

This time Borso took the astrolabe, and held it with an appropriate decorum.

—

It was a Friday. Tonight they were not entertaining outside guests. Borso was simply family now, Bianca was in and out as usual, and Celia had the two children, Lucia and baby Piero.

All had arrived early, and had enjoyed the wine, Celia included.

Celia was sitting up at that same wooden stool she sat on that first day a year ago, but now it was in the dining space. Soon she would move, guessed Gian. She would want to feed her baby. For this one she had not found a suitable wet-nurse.

"I had another wild dream last night," she said.

"And this time ... ?"

"I was in a faraway land, where happiness was everywhere, the Sun shone not too hot, the streets were laid in grass that stayed green and never wore down. Everyone spoke in poetry."

"Where was that?"

"If I knew that I should try to go there."

"And would you walk or ride, or go by galleon?"

"Riding a horse isn't something I've yet learned." She had arrived from Genoa into Panzano on Gian's horse, seated behind.

"By ship?"

"I would need to walk."

"Some day I will persuade you onto the high seas."

The table was set. Bianca entered with a soup and ladled it out for all.

"What have we today, Bianca?" asked Gian.

"Melon and meat broth soup," she said with a grin.

"That's a new one."

"My mother taught me. For only a few weeks the melons are ripe, so I watch the markets. It has gooseberries and whole grapes, too, and egg and grated cheese."

"So it's a fruit, or it's a meat soup?"

"It's both. Mum said the Pope has it."

"Good enough," said Gian. Let's eat." Bianca sat for a short while with them, then left.

Celia, however, picked up the baby and relaxed comfortably to suckle him.

"Last week, Celi, you dreamed you could understand other people's minds," said Gian. "Their true thoughts leaked out, and you captured some."

"Yes, I did, and that was scary. When I realised what those thoughts were, it was horrible. They said pleasant things to me, but they were thinking how boring and irritating I was to them. One wished I were dead. When I knew both their spoken words to me and their inner thoughts about me, it left me sorely conflicted and confused."

"But it was not true, was it?" asked Borso.

"No. But what if it were?"

"And that is the big question. What is the truth?"

"Sometimes," said Celia, "what we are told is a fact, we find later is not. Our Senator in Genoa was a noted orator, who preached the values of honouring our families, and protecting our children and women from harm. He was very popular. One day his glamorous wife disappeared and in public he grieved. They found her body much later buried in the forest. He had beaten her and killed her, and he was eventually judged guilty."

The baby grew restless.

Gian was familiar with Celia's searching always past the apparent and towards what was further beyond. Back in Genoa, quite apart from the arrangements between their families, he and Celia had tortured negotiations, arguments, on how important was the truth. Had he not accepted her demands that he too must be fearless in discovering truth in his own life and in the vision of his telescope, then she would not be his wife.

It was a bargain he had accepted.

"In every culture, such things are hidden."

"How can you say that? I wish for a life of more fairness."

"I never have told you much of my travels, have I?" said Borso.

"Gian told me you had been to Constantinople."

"I have been to Persia, far past Constantinople."

"Oh Borso, tell us all of it."

Borso didn't answer. He poured himself a wine.

Bianca reappeared. More food was coming. Borso jumped up to help clear away the soup bowls, and he placed out regular plates in readiness.

In the centre, Bianca put a bowl of a rich red sauce, and grated parmigiano. A heavy pot of ravioli followed. Gian raised his eyebrows at her. "The pasta? Just yesterday I made it," she said.

"Yes, but what's the red?"

"Tomato," she replied. "From the Spanish America Mexicana."

"I thought tomato was a decoration. Poisonous," said Gian.

"Well, they were in the big Bologna market yesterday. I bought them, I tasted them, and I am healthy," she joked. "Signor, you try that red sauce. You will like it."

Seated again, Borso started. "When I was seventeen, I had finished my schooling, in Venice. One day, without telling my father, I went aboard a galleon and asked them to take me on as a junior sailor. I planned to learn fast and to improve my ranking. I was fit, I was intelligent, and I wanted adventure. Out of Venice, adventure means Constantinople."

"Con. Stan. Tin. Ople." Celia closed her eyes. "Exotic."

"We sailed down to pass the south of Greece, but we suffered a severe storm, and we were beaten southward, managing with difficulty to take shelter at Crete. This was a little before the current siege of Crete by the Turks, but the Turk warboats were already being aggressive. Our ship was not armed enough to try fighting our way out. Then when the weather calmed, the Turks prevented us leaving until three weeks later.

"I said 'us' but unfortunately five of the healthiest young men were detained by the Turks as bounty. They sold us at an auction aboard one warboat, and then they shipped us on to Constantinople as slaves. We laboured, we climbed into the sails, we helped in the food galley. I learned to be the knot counter in the log rope thrown and dragged overboard to measure our speed. We also took turns rowing when the wind dropped."

No one moved. The others at dinner had stopped their eating, spellbound. Borso had been with Cassini for more than a year, but never had he told his story before.

"The five slaves lived in one cell in Constantinople for two weeks. I saw nothing else of the city. We didn't have enough to eat, and less water to drink.

"I was then scrubbed and auctioned again, in a public sale yard where animals were also sold. They sailed us along the south coast of a mighty inland sea, called Black, and put us ashore at the eastern end at a ruined place named Trebizond with still a fine old harbour.

"For five weeks, this time fed properly, two of us walked beside a camel caravan from there across mountains to Isfahan in Iran, in Persia. They roped our wrists to the camel saddle, so we couldn't escape."

"Borso!"

"A month after arriving in Isfahan, I was a third time sent to sale. My new master was a kindly trader who organised caravans both East and West from Iran. He held me no malice. Slaves were a normal fact in his life. He expected me to do service, but I was not maltreated. After a time, I ate with the family, and I was entertained sometimes with the hookah, a smoke of dreams."

The infant was feeding drowsily again. "Borso," Celia said in a soft voice, "Did Isfahan live in peace and happiness?

                                    Cassini's Vision

Was the weather comfortable? Was Isfahan always fertile and green? And do the Isfahan people speak in poetry?"

"I can give you two answers, Signora. Isfahan was just like here. The second answer is this: Isfahan is so different from here that I could take a year to explain it. Both answers are true."

No pasta, no Mexicana red sauce remained.

"And could you know someone else's thoughts there?"

"No. I said Isfahan is like here."

"Borso, I want the year of stories. I want the second answer." Her eyes had tears.

Borso stared long at Celia.

—

"This time," said Celia, "I want to hear more of Borso's Isfahan. Tell us how they get married, and love each other. It is a subject dear to my heart these days."

Bianca took away the Friday plates, a meal of a wild hare she had bought at today's market.

"Well, you tell me firstly what you think love and marriage must mean."

"What they must mean? Borso, I can tell you what their formal meaning is in our Italy, and I can tell you what they mean to me. But what they must mean necessarily? Must? I am not so sure of that."

"Here in Italy," broke in Gian, "marriage is public—a public family contract. We live together with the Church's stamp and blessing upon us. We are commanded to not love others except by our marriage vows."

"Why?" asked Borso.

"Because that is what God decrees. Or so they tell us. And also because we need to know who should deserve to inherit our wealth, our cows or our castle."

"No, that's not the meaning of marriage. To me, it is a pact of love and commitment between us because we choose it." Celia was looking at Gian. "It's simple."

"In Isfahan, they too have marriage between a man and a woman. And yet the loves and lusts of both men and women are not recognisable if we look through an Italian Catholic person's eyes.

"Under Mahomedan law, all the men may take more wives than one, up to four. The only condition is that he needs the wealth to support his wives. With many wives, a man gets many children, and becomes blessed by their God Allah, and is favoured by the king for the count of boys.

"The women may have only the one husband. And I observed that the several wives of one man were scarcely ever friends in any way with each other."

"True?"

"True. The men also expect in their afterlife that they may enjoy with delirious lust any concubines or other women as they please. I heard nothing of the like for women in their heaven, if they have one."

"Not fair!"

"In Iran, an industry of public prostitutes flourishes, protected by the king and by the law."

"But that's sinful, fornication?"

"The Iranian men respect their whores. They believe any slight sin in enjoying a woman is forgotten by bathing with cold water. Simple."

"Oh. And the women accept these versions of love?"

"The free girls are highly willing to dance with their bodies close to naked at parties and ale houses, writhing with wanton lewdness to provoke their men. The wives sometimes join these dances, but their husbands are not very approving. The men take hemp medications to enhance their lusts and the vigour of their member to make answer to the seductions of their women.

"And I forgot, the king and his ministers have more privilege than that. The king takes a harem of many wives and hundreds of concubines, and he imprisons them with more severity than in our convents of nuns.

"I forgot more. Slaves may be mated by their masters at any time. That's not any sin at all."

"Borso, I am shocked."

Gian tried to interpret her face, but despite her words the face was not giving much away.

She was feigning. This was not the Celia he loved for her imaginative passions. By now she had heard and savoured every last adventure of his grand tour, except not yet all of Venice.

"You wanted to know the truths of another land," said Borso. "Celia, I told you what I found there. Would you wish to choose their reality or your own?"

"You told us also that Iran is no different from Italy," she said.

"They love each other, they have children, they have successes, they make mistakes, they cherish their families. They do their best to live worthy and happy lives together. That sounds the same as here."

"The nuns who taught me had a further version," she said. "They thought I should join them in their convent. Within their walls a woman's chastity was safer. We would be the brides of Christ maintaining our virginity unbroken as a gift for our collective celestial spouse."

"Is a collective heavenly spouse different from the four wives of the Isfahan men?"

"Stop. I'm talking convent. Only if we died intact here could our sacred marriage be consummated. The monastic walls ensured our immaculate bodies would be preserved forever, because, they say, the female sex is weak and needs protecting."

"You rejected that." It wasn't a question. But it was a provocation. Therefore, yes it was a question.

"It was an offer just for women. What truth could ever be in that?" She waved her hand, dismissed the idea.

"And," she finished with a vehemence, "Italy has too many convents now. What God would create women with intelligence and lust and beauty, and then want so many locked away?"

"Well," teased Borso, "none of these visions of marriage and loving is the version of Venice. The Venice where I come from."

Venice, mused Gian. Yes, Venice. Venice indeed was different again. What was the truth? What was love?

They must talk Venice.

—

Each Tuesday morning now, Celia went to town. It was a lengthy walk, about two miles, and Gian worried that she would not be safe.

"I'll ride in and take you," he had offered, and he had collected her a few hours later. After the first three weeks, Celia had decided that walking was fine. Unless it was raining, in which case being fetched on horseback would be appreciated, please.

"I will buy a concealable dagger in Bologna. Simply a precaution."

The Bologna school of art had started in the previous century, and had thrived guided by the Carracci painters. From across Italy, the courts, the princes, the Cardinals and the churches had all commissioned and bought high numbers of Bolognese paintings. And Roman and Venetian artworks too, and from Florence and Naples. This in an Italy always at war, with itself, with Spain, with Germany.

Italy's prolific and profitable days were fading, but there were new markets opening, exports into France, and the rest of Europe.

"So that's our predicament right now," she said to Gian. "We painters must start considering business as well as our art." She was naked as a modern school painting, with a token modesty cover that was falling aside. Celia was propped on an elbow and lying on his bed.

  Cassini's Vision

"Our school teaches us styles and techniques that are more beautiful than anyone has ever painted before. They love that I have joined them. However, it is painfully clear I still have much to learn."

"Such as?"

"Like choosing subjects for my art that the marketplace wants and will pay for. I have painted locations I chose, but buyers want portraits and pious scenes. Or big historical dramas. My ships and forests and streets of Genoa aren't what I need to paint now."

Beautiful examples of galleons and streetsides still hung in the portego.

Also on the wall was an eccentric miniature triptych of three views of a circular gate in a forest glade, an intricate and winsome work with no title and no price. Gian had spied her several times standing in silence in front of that piece, and his soul had warned him not to ask. No one else had asked.

"They do like," she added, "that I have appeared in Bologna from nowhere, but that I arrive with existing skill and expertise, and a portfolio already building. It was my grandmother's genius," she boasted. "I owe her this, and I will have her proud of me."

"It is my business and my talent to be proud of you first," he said, and rolled towards her with intent.

Genova Goddess.

Out of nowhere, she said, "Will you take me to Venice one day?" and she kissed him like a crazy woman.

Venice? He hadn't mentioned Venice. But yes, Venice.

—

He never volunteers to speak of "his Isfahan", Celia pondered. But he never demurs if I press.

The family was enjoying Bianca's Friday blancmange pie with milk, rice, chicken and saffron.

The whole meal, all courses, cold, utterly attractive, was laid out together on the table, and Bianca had retired down to her kitchen.

Three heavy and very bright candles in a new candle-holder lit the table. Tonight the Cassinis were enjoying their new beeswax lighting.

"My life's personal passions are art and poetry," she said, apropos of nothing.

It was warm, and, though without a feeding child tonight, she wore light indoor clothes that revealed more of herself than often.

"Your life's personal burdens are young Lucia and Piero," Gian laughed. The toddlers were becoming a threat to the quiet of the house, he had earlier quipped.

"I'll accept that, thanks. I wanted to ask Borso about painting and poetry in Iran."

"Iran has no painting."

"How can that be?"

"The Mahomedan religion forbids images of anything living."

"I could never paint there?"

"Not any leaves, trees, birds. No people."

"Oh, dear. I don't understand a belief system that shuns God's beautiful creatures like that."

"Well, what are beliefs?"

I won't answer that, she thought. "Too hard, Borso."

Pause.

"Are they allowed poetry?"

"The Iranians love their poetry. Every corner, every market, every gathering has a poet entertaining the crowd. The poets have their own standard dress, a cap and a long white open coat. The king employs ceremonial poets. Any marriage has its poet. Celia, you tell me, what makes for a correct piece of poetry?"

"Well, if it rhymes well, that's a strong component. It should have an aesthetic and regular rhythm to the syllables, the meter. But it is important it says something that has fine meaning. Also, something magical is in a poem that says, this is not prose, a different nuance lies behind the words."

"Well, let me list your points for you. In Iran the poets will keep to a strict rhyming. But they are annoyingly poor at maintaining a balanced meter. Some poetry has a quality message, an eloquence and a wisdom, but much is a bit trite, and a lot is copied. Poetry is a widespread entertainment that all the people enjoy, down even to the simpleton. Everyone just knows it's poetry, and not any ordinary spoken story."

"Having said that," he continued, "there live some fine original poets in Iran, and some well regarded classic Iranian and Arabic lyric poems. I have not, however, seen any of these masterpieces translated to Italian or French or English.

"So, my basic report for you on poetry in Iran is this: they have plenty of it, and they love it."

"You speak Iranian?"

"Farsi? Persian? Yes."

"Borso, you have to find us some epic Iranian poetry."

Poetry. Find me poetry.

—

Cassini looked from atop his tower across the Villa complex.

Life in the Panzano Villa for the professor-in-residence and his young family had settled to a regular rhythm.

On most clear nights, Gian would spend his time with the telescope. Once in a while, Borso would, under guidance, take a shift at observation, only calling for Gian if there was something unexpected.

Cassini gained a reputation for the quantity and accuracy of his astronomical recordings. His lectures on findings in the heavens were well attended and respected. He pursued his studies in Bologna.

Celia's two children by now spent most of each week living elsewhere with their balia, their wet-nurse. Otherwise, Celia painted. With Bianca in the house, she no longer needed to cook. House administration tasks? No, Celia was a painter.

Gian loved Celia earnestly, shared her bed with enthusiasm, acted critic on her paintings, treasured that she challenged him to be his most competent, enjoyed her intensity. And he, the practical one of the marriage, did the house administrative jobs, paying, ordering, correspondence, with Borso finishing some of the detail.

Borso proved a capable technician in making and modifying the telescopes, and regrinding some precious lenses. He built props for Cassini's lectures to impress theatre students. For Malvasia, Borso oversaw construction of new stables for two or three horses, pleasing both Malvasia and Cassini, as it made riding to town and back easier. He was teaching Celia to ride. Borso also kept supervision on the local gardener the Marquis had employed.

From his tower, and warmed by the Sun in a cloudless sky, Cassini looked out. The Villa horse was whinnying in the distance. A Cardinal client was leaving through the far gateway. The trees were growing now to be showing above the wall tops and to the rooflines. Smells of a meal cooking wafted in the wind from his kitchen not far away.

A single sneeze caught him by surprise. It was pollen time.

Was he happy?

He should be.

Life was rural. Life was scientific, with a reputation. Life was family, wife and two children. Life was stable.

How long would it last?

The Marquis was his patron, but there would be no rich court patronage in this scenario, no apparent opportunity for academic advancement. Nearby Bologna was known to be jealous of its plum jobs; outsiders seldom were admitted.

—

Celia was excited. At Carnival time, Gian treated her to the promised tour, north to Venice. For the nine days, if there were any children problems, Bianca would attend.

Borso? Borso, the Venice man, would be their Venice guide, and he would be delighted.

Gian made the preparations, arranged accommodation, sent letters.

"Celi, be honest, speak the truth, don't hide the awkward, be brave, look further because you will indeed see more. Your words, remember?"

"Yes, I've heard all that before." She smiled.

"Listen to me. There is a crucial moment of my past that I want to show you. I hadn't told you. You will find more than you expect."

"And you won't tell me what? Well, let me make my own Venice request too. Arrange me a meeting with Arcangela Tarabotti. She is at the convent of Sant'Anna in Castello. The woman is growing to be my heroine."

"Who tells you of this Tarabotti?"

"The women at the Bologna Women's Art Collective on my Tuesdays in town."

They rode, Celia too, stopping at an inn for the first night. By the second night they had left the horses, and were lodged in a modest apartment on a Venice canal—the same canal, he said.

Borso became the gentleman guide, familiar with the places, with the unexpected back ways, and with the beautiful. The gondoliers' slang he was fluent in, and he knew exactly when to sit around to best watch the street events and the overdressed and underdressed revellers.

Murano glassworks occupied a full day. Once across the water, Celia became lost in a heaven of skill and beauty and colour.

The unattractive Sant'Anna Benedictine Convent they found the following day, at the far end of Venice, alongside its church with its tall steeple. At the outside, the convent was a solid stone building of few windows, yielding no secrets on what lay within. The gondola approached at the only gateway visible. Celia was admitted and the strong gates clanged and were re-locked.

"I'll walk the laneways," he had told her. "There are some memories there for me." Then he would wait at the gate.

When she emerged, Gian had his feet dangling in the water beside the convent gate.

"Take me away," she whispered. "Hurry, please." Eventually, anxious, they managed to hail a gondola. "I need to smuggle these papers away before I am spotted."

They settled together, facing forward, and the boat lurched away.

"The nun is a genius and a firebrand. One bitter, angry woman. Her superiors know she is writing again, and they want her material banned by the Vatican.

"The pages I have here are her complete new book. I'm to bring this in secret to the Women's Collective."

"Why do you say she is angry?"

"Tarabotti has no religious vocation. She hates being locked up. Most of Venice's three thousand nuns have no vocation, she says. Their families force them into the nunnery, because society has too many girls.

"Men ensure women don't receive an education, that's her point. Men put women away, and then judge them as ignorant, that's her point. Men want these women to be virginal and pure, but the same men have no intention of choosing that chasteness themselves, that's her anger."

　　　　　　　　　　　Cassini's Vision

"Celia, you run a dangerous errand! Will you publish this book?"

I don't know, she realised. The Collective women need to read it. Tarabotti called it *Paternal Tyranny*.

—

Would Celia publish that document? Gian didn't know either.

Her words came back: You promised me.

Some decisions take time.

And the canal waters still stank.

Borso was promising to get them all into the famed mask ball on their last day in town.

But it was the day before their last that Gian dismissed Borso to visit his old family and friends.

Gian and Celi took a gondola again, and as on each earlier day she had fretted at the unsteady ride on the water.

This was the surprise event.

To Mme Anjelica.

To talk.

It was the biggest risk Giovanni had ever imagined exposing his marriage to. He knew it was outrageous. It was never done, ever.

The first reply from Venice was, "preposterous, not done. Your wife?"

And then Anjelica had sent the Signor professor Cassini a second message, a long one—she had changed her mind. She agreed. She remembered him well. Anjelica was delighted indeed.

This afternoon, at the grand waterside palace of Mme Anjelica, Celia learned more than carnival revels, more than exquisite art, more than proud trading empires. Celia learned whence was born the loving heart of her mate.

"Another most amazing woman. I need courage," she said, as she settled into the gondola.

Enigmatic, he thought.

"Life is magical, she tells me. But it takes great courage."

A new message.

They sat in silence as the gondola swayed slightly, lurched a little, returning them without hurry, as requested, past other people's homes, stone bridges, quaint apartments, past tiny chapels, ostentatious mansions and fashion sellers, to their lodging.

It takes great courage.

"You never told me."

"I did."

—

"The soup, Signora, it's French," proclaimed Bianca, carrying it in with pride.

Signora Celia looked at it. It was like any soup. "What's French in this soup? It is beef."

And beef soup is perfect for tonight, she thought.

"Ah, Signora, it's the chervil. I put the herb in, the 'erb, at the last minute. It's very delicate. My market woman assures me it's French."

Nothing was amiss with Bianca's French soup. It was agreeable soup. It was soup. Bianca was thanked for her soup.

"Borso," said Celia, "tell us about Isfahan soup. Isfahan food. Your promised year of Isfahan stories is not over yet."

He paused a while, as often he did.

"The most ordinary food in Iran is plau, plain rice cooked or soaked in water."

She crinkled her nose.

"They eat rice with all their meals, on all their plates. Often they have it with boiled mutton."

"Still uhk. White and brown."

"No, often the rice is coloured. Pomegranate juice is common, or cherry or saffron yellow. Sometimes green, but I don't know what they use for that."



Cassini's Vision

"All on the one plate?"

"And I have seen that, too.

"They don't grow much wheat, hence as a rule their bread is from their rice. Some bread called barbari is flattened, about three fingers thick and two handspreads long. And lawash is often not leavened, quite thin, sometimes like a thick paper. Or it could be to a finger thickness. None of the bread there looks like our breads."

"What about their meats?"

"They don't like small birds. But plenty of fowl, partridges and pheasants. Meat is plentiful and not expensive, but still they don't eat much meat. They would prefer cheese and fruit. The Persians are outstanding gardeners, and many vegetables and fruit are grown at each household."

"To drink?"

"Water."

"They did," he continued, "bring coffee or cahwa in from Egypt. They burn the little beans in an iron pan until black, beat them to a powder, and boil that in water. I wasn't keen on their coffee. It tasted of burnt crust. But they say it reduces the romantic urges and therefore produces fewer children.

"And wine. Their religion forbids alcohol. But the Christian Armenian and Georgian immigrants make the wine, and it's cheap. No surprise, the Iranians drink a lot of that wine, except the Hatzi don't, those who have gone on pilgrimage to Mecca. The rest drink well, assuring their God they themselves did not make this wine."

"But that's ..." started Celia. She stopped.

"I've not told you yet of the other intoxicants. Many use tobacco. They prefer European tobacco if they can find it, Inglis Tambaku, but when they prepare their own they don't dry it out well as the Europeans do. I don't know why they don't learn. Many draw their tobacco smoke through water in a hookah jar, which I have never seen done here. Or they try hemp. Ah, that smell!

"Iran has an abundance of offioun, opium. They press it into pills the size of a pea, and swallow two or three. It makes them sleepy and as though drunk. The offioun is widespread, and I saw it in Constantinople and into India."

"You took your sample of this offioun?" she probed. Stir some mischief!

"Yes. I sometimes took leave of this world and sailed among the stars." He stood and twirled, rotated his eyes, and grinned.

"Take me to the stars," she said.

—

The following morning, Celia was first to family breakfast. Bianca had set out a food selection in her usual way. Those who wanted any breakfast could arrive in their own time, choose their needs, and leave as they wanted. There were fruits today, and a bowl with oats and a jug of cream.

Borso came in. He had been in the kitchen, helping Bianca unpack and store a food delivery.

"Celia," he said, "maybe you could be gentler with our Bianca."

Oh?

"She cried last night. The soup was not a huge feast meal. But it was still special. She was trying to please us. Her friends at the market had tutored her, and they wanted her to report back on how successful the soup was."

"Oh, I'm so sorry. I didn't mean to shame her."

"Well, she was upset. She couldn't face going to market this morning, so she sent a messenger."

"I must talk with her."

"Yes. And check your cream. I expect it is yesterday's."

   

# Bologna

*The University of Bologna*
*1650*


*To Signor Giovanni Cassini*
*of Panzano Observatory*

*Our University prides itself on being the oldest University in the world.*

*Signor Cassini, this University recognises your learning and your reputation in the disciplines of Astronomy, Mathematics and Engineering.*

*We hereby invite you to occupy the Chair of Mathematics and Astronomy at Bologna.*

*As you will know, this position is vacant because of the sad passing of Father B. Cavalieri. In Father Cavalieri's time with us, he set a high standard of learning, research and lecturing. We are confident you are an eminent candidate to continue this tradition in our venerable institution.*

*You may rest assured that this offer to you has the knowledge and blessing of our board member Senator Marquis Malvasia, Director of Panzano Observatory where you are at present employed.*

—

Cassini was still young. The new stipend was generous. The professorial posting did not include any palazzo, despite that around Bologna there stood many palaces and mansions, and some exceedingly ostentatious ones. With a few negotiations by the influential Malvasia, however, the Cassinis were soon living in a major terrace house, four storeys, and with an inner courtyard to one side.

Gian's requirement had been that there must be a suitable roof access at the rear to allow him to use a modest telescope above their new home. Two observatories and one home telescope should suffice for the most fanatic of astronomers!

He was still astonished at the University's offer and his new appointment. Their requirement that he swear to the Catholic religion was no problem, but their usual reluctance to appoint someone not Bologna-born was waived for him. It was the advantage of having powerful friends. Or one in particular.

"This rather eclipses our home at Panzano." Celia beamed.

They were standing in the kitchen at the back beyond the courtyard.

Until she employed kitchen or maid staff, Celia would need to master enough of this kitchen to feed the house. Men don't cook—unless they are cooks, chefs. This was more kitchen than she had grown up with, more kitchen than they had in Panzano.

The kitchen had an extremely high ceiling, so that it occupied two storey levels, ground floor and first-floor mezzanine. Adjacent to the kitchen were the regular food storage room and a cool protected room for careful preparations or for perishables such as cheeses.

There was an oven with an iron door, and an open fire as well. Some fittings remained from the previous owners. Mobile iron arms above the fire that could support cauldrons. Some hooks still hanging high up. And a stone trough that could have water available to it. They would still need more sideboard space and a strong centre table. Also, they were short of utensils and plates, unless these were stowed aside somewhere.

A narrow pinewood staircase in the kitchen ascended to the household sala above, their dining room, two storeys up, past the mezzanine. Under the stair was a space that might serve as a sleep area for a kitchen maid or cook.

A bathing tub stood not far from the steps. "Look what we have here," said Gian. "We might have to fill this for a full bathe sometimes. It could be each autumn and each spring?"

"Oh, and who heats the water and fills the tub?"

"When we employ some staff."

"My mother thought bathing was unhealthy. But a tub might make hair washing easier."

Two bells were high on the inside wall. "Two? One is from the chainpull outside the gate. The other?"

"I guess the other is rung from the dining room upstairs. We can check later."

Gian and Celia walked through the several service rooms that ran alongside the courtyard. Windows looked into the courtyard and garden. Across the yard in the far corner near the kitchen, a handpump stood over the water well. A modest plot growing vegetables wanted attention.

They continued forward to stand a little inside their solid main doors, two head-heights high, with their security grill. The huge hall they were now in, their portego, was the width of their house, and it had generous windowing into the best aspect of the garden courtyard. Thick wooden beams crossed the room to support its ceiling, creating a strong but elegant pattern of light along the length. Only the house staircase broke the clean expanse of the portego floor.

"We could stage a banquet here, or we might squeeze in a social ball." He looked in awe.

"Husband, my dear," she mocked, "don't reach above your station. Not yet. I thought this new job was for science and mathematics, discovering the new and unexpected. Not for civic strutting."

He grinned, admonished.

"And in any case, this entrance hall is too, what shall I call it, too—too absolutely fabulous." She flung her arms wide.

"That's a wild assessment."

"It will suit a display hall for the Bellini Art." Her artwork she kept in her name of origin.

What is truth? he thought. What is the right way? Can it be right a woman bids to stand tall as her man?

"We have rooms enough for a work studio further back, before the kitchen, but an impressive gallery that every visitor must come through is the obvious use for this. You can still hold any event you wish here, but a gallery needs the walls. These walls."

This woman, yes. It had been a pact. It remained a pact. Just now, it wasn't a fact; it was a decision.

This transaction. Familiar. Is the truth, the dream, again beyond what we had thought?

"Gian, I have such a substantial collection of my work that I have never sold, not yet ever exhibited. Thank you." She wrapped her arms about him, with that abandon befitting mates.

Giovanni and Celia were ready for Bologna.

—

It was a week later that Celia opened the gates to let in a tearful Bianca.

"Signora, Signora, I have nowhere to live."

Celia and Bianca walked back into the kitchen. Pots remained unwashed; the place was untidy. Some embers were still smoking in the fireplace, smelling just of ash.

"Oh, Signora," wailed Bianca, looking around. This was a bigger kitchen than at Panzano.

Celia added light twigs to get a tiny fire going, and hung a kettle over it.

"May I?" Bianca rearranged the kindling and the flame flared.

Celia imagined she was not embarrassed.

"You're hungry, too?"

Bianca nodded. Celia returned with a jar of cakes she had bought at the market yesterday.

They sat together a while, and Bianca took a cake.

"Signora Cassini, I never did tell you. My mother died last year. I have no home."

"Oh, Bianca, I'm so sorry. I didn't know."

"When I left your Panzano house, I spent a few days with my brother and his wife. She is a mean woman. There was no welcome for me."

"So where are you living now?"

"I slept in the Panzano stable most nights. I wasn't discovered."

Celia paused.

Bianca took another cake.

"And you have no work, no house that will employ you?"

"No. There is not much option around Panzano."

"We assumed you would stay local with your family, and make new working arrangements."

"Signora, was my work good?"

"Yes, of course."

Bianca's skill with her dinners had grown well in her Panzano years. Without question her service could suit the Bologna life well.

"I could be your kitchen cook here?" Bianca looked around. No one was putting love or care in here.

"I think we might accept that. But as at Panzano, I am not planning on a separate maid for food service. It would be all one job just as before, cook and service."

Bianca nodded.

"I can work for you here. You would be proud of your kitchen and its dinners."

Bianca thought a while longer.

"But, Signora, one more thing I would ask. At Panzano I was asked sometimes to eat with you all, when the family was together. And even when you had worthy visitors. It shouldn't be my job, Signora. I am the maid, not the family. I want to be a proper maid and know my own place in the household. I was not raised to eat with fine people. It makes me unhappy."

"Hmm. Well then, when would you start?"

Bianca looked to the floor. "There's nowhere to return to," she said.

"I have a condition as well, Bianca. Your food has been fine for us at Panzano, both the ordinary meals and the bigger Friday dinners. I will trust you to do the same here, and even better. But here at Bologna there may be times when we will have some much longer and more formal meals, even a banquet once our life becomes stable. Can I have your agreement that on some occasions you would accept that I hire an outside chef and staff to cope with more major events? They would be in your kitchen. That would not be frequent, I expect."

Again Bianca nodded.

She doesn't have any other option, realised Celia. Perhaps we don't either.

"Done. I will make the same wages arrangement for you as before. As at Panzano I will pay all the food bills."

Gian would.

     Cassini's Vision

"Now let me show you where you can sleep." She led Bianca to the alcove under the pinewood stairs.

Painting was more rewarding than domestic matters.

"Oh, and Bianca, I will need a housemaid soon too, but for the moment, can you at least keep drinking water in our rooms, and water and basin for washing? And can you mind the chamber pots?"

—

"I'm back in Venice," was Borso's first reaction. This building felt like some of his childhood.

"The portego! But you have it crosswise. To me, a portego runs down the house, windows each end."

"We are in Bologna," she said. "You want to go back to Venice?"

"I don't."

"Correct. We need you here."

Borso had been doing finishing-up jobs in Panzano.

He peered through into the courtyard. "You could play games with a youngster in there. Under watch."

"That may be. I have a couple. Or three now."

"The yard needs water and a cleanup, though. And some pruning. I could contract Malvasia's gardener to come here every week or so. How far away is our town water?"

"Two hundred paces only. Though we do have our own well," she replied. "Over there. And a hand pump that can put water in the tank above the kitchen."

"But come and check my new botega. It's my painting room." It was a mess, some materials still boxed and some scattered, easel needing repair after transporting.

"You may need a hand with that."

"And come here. This room is to be my studiola. No painting, just thinking and planning. Resting." A sofa was in there, and a desk.

She had a gleam in her eye. "I'll show you more. Come."

She led him into the kitchen.

"Your studio rooms are alongside the maid quarters
and kitchen," he said. He was puzzled.

"It'll do. At Panzano I had a lot less room than that.
And here I face out on that courtyard."

"Sure. Beautiful. Except for Monday washdays, I
suppose."

"I need a housemaid first."

She showed him up the maid's delivery steps, only as
far as the mezzanine. "Follow me." They climbed through a
low doorway,

This woman behaves as a scheming schoolgirl.

Celia walked him forward to the mezzanine front room
with the street windows. She grinned.

"You might rather like this room, it's yours."

"I will. Now if you please don't mind, I need to use an
ordinary stairway to bring my belongings up."

# The Heavens

Seasons came and passed. Bologna life became settled. It was now the week before Christmas.

At the University, a messenger arrived for Cassini from Panzano Villa. The Marquis wanted Cassini to visit the Observatory that same evening.

Cassini's professorship at Panzano was not terminated when he moved to Bologna two years ago. At Panzano, he still did significant planetary work. They were preparing a massive ephemerides publication.

Today was unexpected.

Gian had a private student with him. "Beringelli, I must depart. Sorry."

The lad was no fool. "Well, we must be suspicious that something in the night sky is interesting, Signor. Can I be impertinent and ask to go with you?"

"Well, I don't have enough reason to refuse. We would walk. It's about two miles hence."

The two walked to Cassini's home to make domestic apologies with Celia and the three children, and then set out for Panzano.

"Signor, thank you. I am taking it as an honour to accompany you."

"Neither of us knows what we are walking to."

"Signor, my father spoke often of your fame in the years you lived at the Observatory. Today at your

Observatory there may be something new in the heavens. Why else would they want you there?"

"Could be I forgot to pay my bills?"

"Signor, please don't be gruff with me. I know the Marquis still works with you and respects you. This is something big tonight. If it's a night of history, I want to share in it."

Beringelli wanted something, perhaps? Perhaps not. Take his enthusiasm at its obvious meaning.

They walked on through the cool afternoon.

At the Villa, they were welcomed in by Malvasia and the Duke of Modena to a fast meal before darkness fell.

"We have una cometa," Malvasia said. "Tycho Brahe reported a Great Comet in 1577. Then another comet appeared in 1618 and all Europe saw it. Now us. We have this one."

He was not claiming it as his own—it was to be a joint find. The Marquis still believed in his young astronomy professor, and gave him the credit.

Still an asset.

The night was cold but the sky was favourable. This tiny speck in the telescope showed its mane, but it was not "great". The men felt no cold.

"Those two stars beside it were last night twice that far away."

"We don't have a name for those stars, but locate them in the constellation for me," asked Gian. During the coming month, we can both study this body."

—

"What is this comet?" she asked when he returned.

"We don't know. Not even where it came from. And we don't know why it has a tail of white hair behind it. Its path agrees with no star or planet."

"The Inquisition hates changes to the Earth and its heavens. Are you intending to publish what you find?"

  Cassini's Vision

"Yes. I must." He sounded tired.

—

Cassini spent the cold winter nights taking accurate comet measurements. Borso and Battista Riccioli often took observation shifts.

"Battista, one day, not regarding our comet, can you show me the gnomon in our Church of San Petronio, the basilica? I have been reading the stored reports in Latin of my predecessors, both Egnatio Danti and Father Cavalieri. Danti built this one long ago."

"Gian, I wish I could show you. But only a few years back the huge basilica was partly rebuilt. The Sun's spyhole is gone—that wall was removed. The tiled floor pattern still remains. So sorry." Battista resumed writing his observation figures.

—

Cassini was struggling to develop a theory on where the comet could have come from. It was measurably beyond Saturn. Astronomical mathematics by now was achieving that kind of accuracy with confidence. But he had still no clear answer on what a comet was.

In proper time, he published his report *De Cometa*, including all detailed trajectory points and timing, in the hope a future mathematician might have better interpretations. He dispatched copies to many of universities and institutes across Europe.

It was in Latin, the international language of the learned. The only scientist Gian had known who wrote in his native language had been his mentor Galilei.

*De Cometa* was Cassini's first major scientific report, and the acclaim was a boon to his own rising reputation and a credit to his University. But it had no answers. The Earth was stationary, as the Inquisition insisted. Heavenly bodies moved around God's Earth. Planets behaved awkwardly. And comets were quite without explanation, assuming the soothsayers were ignored. Astronomers were measuring all the bodies with ever more precision, but the mathematics was not fitting well.

Cassini had a problem. He didn't believe what his own report was saying.

Celia sensed he was troubled, he could tell, but neither talked of it. This conflict he needed to solve in his own way.

—

Cassini visited the renovated basilica. The faint incense of a Mass hung in the air, and a dozen people stood in corners, praying silently. The geometric pattern and the meridian lines still were tiled in the floor, but served no purpose.

He knew the gnomon's early task. Danti's eighty-year-old report was detailed. The calendar Julius Caesar established before the time of Christ had drifted further from the true seasons as the centuries passed. Every fourth year had been a leap year, with February having an extra day. But after many hundreds of years, this formula proved too simple.

Pope Gregory in 1582 reset the New Year date and allowed for different rules to apply to leap years when they were the start of a century. Now the calendar tracked the Sun's seasons far better. However, it was unfortunate, but the Church calculated its grandest feast of Easter not by calendar, but from Moon cycles and March equinox. Determining the exact (new calendar) date of the equinox had become urgent.

Europe had built gnomons inside many major buildings, and the highest was in the Bologna basilica. Danti had made a peep-hole high in a wall, arranged to keep out rain but to let the Sun shine through. A narrow ray of Sun

                                    Cassini's Vision

had shone on the floor tiles. But the Bologna peep-hole was now gone.

Cassini sat on the tiled pattern and meditated there for a long time before strolling home.

"Would the Church like a new gnomon?" Cassini offered to Battista when next they met.

Yes, I believe the basilica council would be overjoyed.

Yes, what would you plan?

Yes, I can raise it next week.

Yes, Gian, the council has approved. Would be elated. Before this Easter?

Gian and Borso inspected and talked and inspected again. His new peep-hole needed to be high, as high as possible. The renovations offered possibility of a much higher hole than the previous.

"So high? Who is going up there?"

"Yes, that high. And you. Climb up there with the builders and make sure it is feasible. Inside and outside. Leave me a mark on where it can be opened."

It proved difficult, but Borso and the builders settled on an acceptable location.

Before ordering a hole in a church roof, the tiled floor symbols had to be re-laid in correct place to match the angle and the sweep of the Sun's ray. Borso constructed a temporary astrolabe style instrument for the task. Gian calculated Sun and season, and together they marked their spot. A lot of reputation rested on this accuracy.

The builders lifted and re-laid the tiles. Then they opened the new Sun hole high on the wall.

It was still three months to wait for equinox.

In late March, Gian started supervising hourly readings for two weeks. The Sun's ray from the tiny hole spread to a large circle of light on the tiles. It blurred only a little at its edges, and it kept moving along the tile at a surprising speed. As equinox time approached, three observers were each recording their separate measurements, trying to smooth away errors in what they judged.

A day after equinox Cassini could pronounce that the event had occurred at a few minutes after 3 pm Bologna time on the yesterday.

But Giovanni Cassini, Chair and Professor of Astronomy, had little need to be just another engineer who could read the equinox precisely. There were other reasons his gnomon was the highest.

—

"Borso, the Earth stays here, steady, and the Sun rises and falls each day. Goes around us. Right?"

The assistant looked puzzled. "Of course."

"Are you sure?"

"... No."

"Why can you be sure and not sure?"

"I wish they don't burn me."

"That's not science, is it?"

"Sure."

"What if instead the Earth was steady and only the Sun goes around us. And then if the planets and that pesky comet went around the Sun and not around the Earth? We do know now the Sun is very large, bigger than the Earth."

"Complicated, Signor. But I must say some of your planet recordings would make more sense. But Signor, I am not the mathematician. You should tell me."

"Borso, think again. What if it was the Sun that stayed motionless? And the planets and the Earth too were circling the Sun?"

"Signor, you know well that Copernicus and your friend Galilei spoke that belief. It did them no favour."

"Could they have been right all along?"

Borso made no answer.

"Come with me tomorrow to the basilica. I plan a new investigation on the Sun's shadow, and it will take a long



Cassini's Vision

time to conclude. We can be safe there, because last year's equinox readings were so well received. Bologna has pride in its research reputation."

—

"Celi, I have a surprise."

"Do I know it already? Is it Friday dinner?"

He was surprised. "Yes, it is. What's your version?"

"That il Guercino is coming to dinner. I'm so excited. How did you score such a prize?"

"Your teacher was working on a commission at the basilica, a huge altarpiece painting. After the architectural changes a few years ago, they are now updating the artwork. The basilica wanted the best."

"He is the best. He paints superbly, and fast. Plus, he is a Bologna man, and high points are scored for that. You know, as our chief teacher he takes so much care with each one of us. I love him."

Gian blinked.

"Well, he has scaffold and trestles all about the main altar at present. Pots of paint around and sheets of cloth over everything. We were the two non-penitents bustling about the place last week. The chief astronomer/engineer of Bologna and the master painter/teacher of Bologna. We both stopped and went out together to find hot drinks at the marketplace."

"He told me, he told me yesterday." She giggled. "Oh Gian, he is so expensive. I could only wish."

Celia consulted with Bianca. What could be a suitable dinner for one very celebrated guest?

Bianca made an offer. Celia made it into an argument. They settled on a calculated and accepted gamble.

"I have last week tried it myself," pleaded Bianca. "They are little white knuckles, chewy dumplings. And they tasted excellent with a cheesy sauce." The sauce was familiar, but those dumplings were of potato.

"Potato is animal fodder," shrieked Celia. "They are roots eaten by Spanish New World indians, and brought here for our cows and pigs."

Celia did agree to sample later Bianca's experimental knuckles, the gnocchi. Two of Bianca's friends showed up as recipe experts. Celia made her tasting—and she approved the gnocchi for Friday.

On Friday late afternoon, Giovanni Barbieri, "il Guercino" the Squinter, appeared at the gates ready for a promised evening of social and comfortable entertainment in the grand hall up in the Cassini residence.

Celia had hung recent works in the portego gallery inside the front doors.

Shortly the Senator the Marquis Malvasia arrived to join them.

"I was not aware an old reprobate like you was coming tonight," said Malvasia. "You remember, I found them first."

Them? thought Celia.

The visitors laughed and embraced.

Malvasia walked along the paintings to admire them. "They're classy," he said. "You teach an excellent academy."

Barbieri spread his arm out in Celia's direction. "When I was a kid, I knew her grandma. Grandma Crovese was an accomplished artist, and rich from it. Our Signora has art in her blood. Celia is an able and fast student. You keep watch on this talent, Count, believe me."

Celia was blushing.

"Hey, Squinter, what's this about? A lot of gore and skulls in this."

"Ask her."

"Sorry, Celia dear, be kind to tell me about this. It's a scene of horrific destruction."

"That's an episode from the Book of the Apocalypse," she said. "The Second Horseman, the red one, bringing widespread war. The final judgement is near, the Armageddon, the end of all this world."

                    Cassini's Vision

"Littered with skulls and limbs. So dark. And the painting is still so bright."

"We see many skulls in the intense biblical art," said Barbieri. "And in the art on lives of the saints. A reminder that Death is always hovering. The hereafter is never far off."

"I don't remember that part in my Bible classes. You're sure it is in the Bible?"

"But I like the painting anyway," he went on. "In my game, Death is a player all the time as well. Celia, talk with me later. I like it."

"Please," called Celia, "we can move upstairs to the master halls. Dinner will wait a while yet, but we need some good wine first. Tonight the fires are alight in both rooms."

She had trouble persuading the Senator. He had moved along to a recent portrait she had made of a well-respected woman in the town. Malvasia stared long at it, pouting, thinking. Then he nodded to himself and followed them up the stairs.

"Are there any of Zeus and Pan, the older religions?"

"The pagan mythologies?" asked Barbieri, slowing his step. "They are a staple. The pagan and the Christian in conflict. The old gods and the Gospel God. Celia has two old mythology works down there, both Venus and one of those with a Cupid. They are on the other wall that you didn't look at. Wonderful. Classy pieces of art. My dear Count, anywhere drama or strife exists, or Heaven or Hell or great love or piety, anywhere there is a lesson to learn in life, we artists are there."

"Oh, a glass of wine, let's have a glass or three of healthy wine."

Celia was not listening. She walked up the steps ahead of the others, and paused at the basin outside the main hall. Her body went through the usual motions of a hand wash, but her mind was elsewhere. She had not been right in keeping her art as Bellini.

Her Bellini reputation was still young. She should sign from now as Celia Crovese, with her true artistic heritage.

The irony hit: she had once thought Gian a Crovese.

But the little potato knuckles waited.

—

The irony that hit Gian later was the ambiguity of her new brand. A Crovese badge for her art would appear to come through his Uncle Antonio Crovese rather than from Celia's own family line.

Celia continued signing her work as Bellini, with a new pride.

The Bellini Gallery flourished.

—

Professor Cassini published his comprehensive report on the gnomon research. With copies dispatched across Europe, it consolidated his reputation as Italy's lead astronomer and as a worthy ambassador for the University of Bologna.

What he omitted from this report, however, was one stream of research still ongoing at the gnomon.

The circle of light thrown on the church floor was large, and clear enough at the edges to record the diameter of the spot on any day at noon. That size of the light circle could change a little day by day, and from that could be calculated the changing distance of the Sun.

The mathematician knew exactly what he was looking for. The Earth could be steady and the Sun circled it, as per tradition, as per Rome, as per Ptolemy. Or the Sun might be still, and a rotating Earth was going around the Sun, as per Galilei's heresy. The Sun's varying distance recorded throughout the year would be a distinctly different pattern for the two cases.

Cassini was recording the width of the Sun's spot each day. And the mathematical result, read from the church's floor, was already clear.

The Earth was circling the Sun.

This was the most tragic truth, the first incontestable and scientific proof, the most dangerous fact that a Papal state Italian Catholic could know.

Borso knew the conclusion.

Celia was terrified. Her artwork was turning to Hades and Armageddon.

And she knew it was her doing.

—

Malvasia had never revealed how he had chanced upon his comet. Long ago it had disappeared from view.

Cassini and Riccioli sometimes spent companion time on one or other of their telescopes, using stratagems to find another comet. Tonight was a cold night, and the instrument was Battista's Divini model. Did the comets all come from one direction?

Battista favoured looking at random for a small object with a hairy tail. But did all comets have a tail? The classic Big Comets of history did, but the Panzano comet's tail had shrunk and then faded. Battista treated comet chasing as light interludes between his other clearer research.

Cassini preferred sketching. He had amassed and catalogued an extensive stockpile of star patterns, some of which his brain would keep in memory anyway. He could reference with ease the old sketches against tonight's viewing.

"Nothing moves. Ever. Or only planets move. There are no comets," muttered Cassini.

Time to go out at risk.

"Tista, I've been curious. In your clerical life, how did you balance your Galilei friendship with your Popeness?"

The Jesuit stopped viewing and sat back. He was under no illusion exactly what Cassini was asking. He had expected this some day, and that some day was now.

"We Jesuits are a powerful army. Our weapons are knowledge, argument, and above all, influential contacts in the world."

Neither spoke for a long while.

"You are sure, aren't you, Giovanni? By now you must be."

Gian nodded. Their eyes did not meet.

"In this world of today, my friend, it is now you who has most knowledge and the highest scientific authority. Our Pope's misguided, Giovanni. The Inquisition is wrong, and the Pope is weak."

"The Inquisition is heavy with Jesuits."

"I agree. It's a mess."

"But why?"

"Those idea wars are being fought for reasons of European and in particular Italian politics. They're fought on wealth and ambition and political prestige. Probably it ever was so."

The rebellious vehemence of this priest of Rome was a surprise to Cassini.

"My dear Giovanni, I have known you a long time. I am another who believes in your integrity and your passion. Why, even your wealthy magician the Marquis trusts you. Still."

"But I am conflicted so."

"And I also. I never told you this, but twice in the last year, I have heard of two Cardinals plotting to bring you down. To discredit your work. To destroy the memory of you. Your investigations are becoming dangerous to the Rome dogma. I have placated them, vouched for you, for your adherence."

Cassini turned aside. "I'm stunned. Am I at that much risk?"

"Well, yes you are. But I have many friends who owe me favours in this world. I suppose I am true to my training! I can help protect us, if you can slowly—slowly, I must repeat—develop your evidence so one day it can be brought out safely into God's good light. As before, please allow me to check over your drafts before you go to publication. Earnestly I want that we should prevail. My friend Galilei missed his step. This time we must not."

We?

"Explain it to me."

Pause.

"The whole Christian story assumes this Earth is centre stage of history's drama. Humans live here, but it's only transitional. We live close to Hell below, but for now we are compelled to live on Earth with its insecurities and its filth. God placed us on Earth, and He watches us always. He invites us to be good and moral—no easy task I admit—and then we will receive our reward and our escape into Paradise. If we fail, if we follow our base natures, we tumble into the permanent pits of the Inferno.

"Two hundred years ago, Dante, a Florence man, put it with such poetry and insight in the Divine Comedy."

"My schoolmasters tried to lead us through the Divine Comedy. It was too much for a boy."

"Go back to it. It is the finest literature in our Italian language, and not Latin. It summarises the Christian world view. One temporary Earth, for Man's testing. Followed by permanent reward or everlasting damnation."

"Yes."

"Gian, this vision leaves no room for Earth not to be centre of the universe. That's the whole problem."

# Huygens

A report arrived to Bologna from Paris that researcher and astronomer Christiaan Huygens had discovered a new body in the heavens. At his home in The Hague he had been observing the planet Saturn, the furthermost of the planets. He found a moon, faint, almost invisible, circling that planet. Luna Saturni, he called it, Saturn's Moon. For now, Huygens was studying in Paris for some months.

Cassini forthwith sent messages to Paris, and then he and Borso made quick preparations to travel. The obliging Marquis supplied three horses from Panzano Villa.

The action was elsewhere. Cassini needed to be there.

"We'll leave after a lunch."

Borso looked alarmed. Cassini was stowing away a substantial wad of money.

"I haven't the time to organise letters of credit on any Paris bank."

"Here," said Borso, "give me half."

The ride as far as Turin was an unremarkable journey. The spare horse, tethered behind, carried more than its third share of the luggage they needed, luggage that included warmer weather clothing for the Alpine climb to come.

Neither man had been to Turin. They found a well-walled city, square, with four controlled gates. Inside, to one side, was a formidable citadel, where the duke and family, usually at war even with the townsfolk, could remain protected.

Gian's thoughts fell back to Antonio's remarks long ago on Venice, unwalled, sitting at sea, and never conquered.

Already here the River Po was wide in many places, ready to weave East, dodging all the cities, Genoa, Milan, Bologna, Mantua, and then flowing to the Adriatic Sea beneath Venice.

On instruction from Celia, they visited the Domo, the Great Church. She wanted a report on the winding cloth reputed to be held there, the burial cloth of Our Lord after his crucifixion. Gian was ambivalent about his mission here, but Celia had been clear.

"That was long past a thousand years ago. History has seen wars, desolations, discontinuities and centuries of barbarianism. It seems unlikely such a thing can have been kept. Can you bring me back some truth?"

The shroud was in keeping in a chapel over the high altar. Only on certain feast days was it brought out for public showing. The unscheduled travellers from Bologna had insufficient influence here for a private exposition. Cassini was relieved.

A new side chapel inside the Domo was half-constructed, intended as a new repository for the shroud. It was of black marble, with fine pillars also of black marble. The new space, if ever finished, should be a more sombre one than the one atop the high altar. The solemnity and grandeur would be a protection for the imagined veracity of the cloth's sacred story.

From Turin, they rose into the Alps. The season was hospitable, and they managed to ride up the formidable Mount Cenis, with only sporadic snow around the top.

"Don't you wish we had mules as the locals have?" asked Borso. "They are so sure-footed."

They crossed the short plateau, and then walked cautiously with their horses down into the Savoy.

The road continued rough and slow, winding, steep at times and narrow, until they emerged finally into Lyon.

The whole journey to Paris took most of a month.

By the time they found where Huygens was staying in Paris, he still had two weeks of his physics studies left to finish. He had not received any message, but was delighted to be receiving a distinguished colleague from afar.

In all Italy, Cassini had splendid instrument makers in Rome, and two colleagues, Malvasia and Riccioli in Bologna. But just the one city of Paris hosted a density of expertise and discussion that Cassini found exhilarating.

Cassini's French language skill was only modest. He kept Borso at his side.

The Dutchman Christiaan Huygens was four years younger than Cassini, and was skilled in astronomy, mathematics, several languages, law, and now physics. He had several respected theses published, one recently released on the intricate calculus of circles. His wealthy father was a diplomat, poet and linguist, who could mix with no effort among the aristocrats and the influential of Europe. It was family friend Rene Descartes who had spotted the mechanical talents of young Christiaan and helped launch a successful career. Huygens was a man with an assured future.

"I made my telescope myself only early this year," said Huygens. "It's four arm-spreads long."

"So long?"

"I was trying to grind the lenses flatter, to keep the distortions lower. And then I needed the length to give me back the magnification."

Cassini still used his Roman telescopes. They were good.

"But why were you looking to Saturn? No one has bothered with Saturn since Galilei saw the side smudges forty years ago. We have been threatened by the Copernican and Keplerian debacle about the Sun."

Huygens did not take the bait.

"Well, these years our telescopes are much better, so several of us started again on Saturn. What were the disappearing parts of Saturn? And we still are not sure. They keep changing shape."

"But what I did see also, was a small star that went from side to side, as though through or behind Saturn. A little later I saw it as a thin ellipse shape movement instead of a line, and I realised it was a tiny planet going around the larger planet. Saturn has a moon, as the Earth has a Moon. Can you believe that?"

Huygens' interpretation of the heavens as he laid it out for Cassini was, without any apology, assuming the heretical belief of the Sun as centre. The little bodies circle the bigger ones. The Sun was the largest, and Huygens' baby planet was the smallest.

Christiaan's easy manner and his impressive family connections opened intellectual opportunities everywhere for him. Cassini immersed himself into the rich world of powerful scientific and social contacts. The French food he might learn to enjoy, but it was not Italian.

Cassini stayed only ten days in Paris. It was the centre of science, and he felt well rewarded for his two months in all away from home. He made plans to visit his new colleague at The Hague in the Netherlands as soon as could be suitable.

Next time he would not ride. He would take a ship from Genoa, and have time to write and study. Cassini had never travelled by ship.

—

Christiaan collected the two Italian travellers from Amsterdam harbour in a hired carriage. Holland was importing horse-drawn carriages from Germany in recent times, and these made short and medium journeys more dignified than they had ever been.

When not abroad, Constantijn, Huygens' father, lived at the family mansion in Amsterdam.

"But since I came of age," said their host, "I have been using our family summer estate at Den Haag as home. I am alone here with two house staff from our family. Also, I have purchased a building nearby where I study and work, and I call that my laboratory."

The Huygens summer refuge by the canal at The Hague was a more modest home than the reported Amsterdam house. "More modest" Gian took to be relative only, and the carriage arrived at a proud brick block of three storeys, standing apart from its neighbours, and surrounded on three sides by the waters of a creatively landscaped small lake on the canal.

The horses drew up along the cobbled trackway, the only access across the lake, to the steps of Christiaan's home. The butler stepped out to help with the travel luggage, and the men went inside, leaving the coachman to the task of turning around his vehicle.

From the entrance, wooden stairs wound up to the chief living hall. Courtesies, small talk and admiration occupied them at first. From the ample windows overlooking the lake and the canal, Gian saw their butler rowing away in a small boat.

Refreshments arrived from the water-level kitchen below. For the three of them, four places had been set.

They heard the boatman returning outside. Christiaan rose. "Tomorrow we visit the laboratory, but we have a guest joining us this afternoon," he said. "She is homesick for some Italian language, and the prospect of Venetian Italian was an opportunity she asked to be allowed."

Borso smartened up. Gian smiled, and nodded at Huygens.

A woman came up the steps and joined them. She was young, neat, modestly dressed, and confident to be meeting the men.

"This is Signorina Martelli, Lorenna Martelli. My colleague from Bologna, Signor Giovanni Cassini, and Borso Gordeo. They will stay here with me for a week."

The butler/boatman carried the first of the luggage up the stairs and further upwards to the storey above.

"Now, the coach will be returning in two hours. Firstly we can lunch, and then I want to take you by carriage and you can see my beautiful city."

Lorenna was a young administration and finance expert employed by old Constantijn. Most weeks she resided in Amsterdam, but on occasion she used lodging arrangements near to the summer house, when she had work here at The Hague.

"She couldn't stay at your house?"

"Oh, never. Not in the Netherlands. The scandal would be a disaster."

Lorenna nodded.

Gian discreetly cocked one eyebrow at Christiaan. He received back a friendly glare.

"But you are a believer?"

"No."

"Actually," Lorenna said, "I don't have any tasks here this week. And in Amsterdam too my contract is almost completed. Today I am here simply for a social visit. I wanted to meet with Christiaan's important visitors. And, I suppose, to be reminded of home."

And so, after their lunch, see The Hague they all did, in modern style and comfort.

"I was talking with her non-stop," Borso said later, "when you two were climbing that monument in town. That woman does know her trade, I think."

"And what trade is that?"

"She has been analysing old Constantijn's assets and their risks. She might be young, but he trusts her. She mapped out some changes to protect his estates in case war returns. They have just had eighty years of religious war right here, and the Peace is only a handful of years old."

"Did she leak you any secrets on his wealth?"

"Not. She would never."

How would Borso know that? In one afternoon?

But Lorenna was one impressive woman.

She would return to Amsterdam after three days. Three days.

Three days.

—

On the walk to the laboratory on their third day, they took the same canal-side path as their return home yesterday.

"She's not there," said Borso.

"Who is not where?"

"On these stone steps down to the water, I saw a fortune teller here last evening. I thought I might pay her to read my future."

"Then likely tonight she would be back," laughed Huygens. "I've seen her before. She is Romani, surely, gypsy."

—

They found Borso sitting with the soothsayer. He had left them earlier in the afternoon.

The two were squatting on the canal steps, eyes closed. They were conversing spiritedly, but not in any familiar language. Gian and Christiaan sat themselves a few steps above, and waited.

It was ten minutes before the woman and her client stopped, and Borso opened his eyes.

"Gentlemen," she said, "I have had wonderful memories with your colleague." But her voice was male, with a Venice Italian accent.

"Borso?" asked Gian.

"The Madame is from Iraq, Baghdad. I knew yesterday. Her clothes, her colours. It was Persian, Farsi, that you heard."

"She has called your cards?"

"Not cards, boss, just my future. It's unnerving."

"Sorry, sirs," she said. Her accent had changed to Bologna.

"Gentlemen," she continued. The voice had shifted to Bologna female.

"Gentlemen, your colleague is from my world. I have been enjoying the reminiscences. He has paid me well."

"She wants to talk with us all," said Borso.

"And I do. I should embrace you all in a short seance tonight."

"Gian?" Huygens sought a confidence. He spoke only the one word.

Her Italian took on another shape. "Sirs, sit closer. We have time. I want to sit with you and my friend Mister Borso. This day is a special moment for you all. I feel that."

Borso sat them closer.

"All of you, show me your hands, your palms." For several minutes, she studied all the palms.

"Now, smell the water. Feel the breeze. Know that the stars press upon your heads."

She lit an incense whose smoke scattered in the late afternoon wind, and she closed her eyes.

"All close your eyes," she said. "Tonight I have messages for you all. The three of you. I do not know which messages are for each. You must listen with care."

There was silence for another minute.

"Two of you will see much water and too much black. And what becomes important will be invisible to you.

"Two of you will be famous, very famous, but you will not be home. To be famous, you will be away, far away from your real home. You will never go home.

"Two of you will find true love. Love that is hard. Love that challenges all you can stand."

Gian shuffled on his cold stone seat.

"And all three of you are on a commission. I know that. And you too must know that. You are all ordained by the universe, by all the stars and planets, to be searchers for the truth, the next truth, the final truth. It will be your own choice to accept your mission."

—

"Giovanni, I haven't told you anything of our talk club."

After his traumatic ritual yesterday beside the canal, Borso the Venice boy now had the day off. He had ventured out alone to explore the canals. Did these waterways have their own mystery?

"Talk Club?" asked Gian.

"It has no name—it's no more than just three friends. We meet every couple of months, usually in Amsterdam and occasionally here."

"In your laboratory?"

"Yes, here or at home. My two colleagues are Rene Descartes and Baruch Spinoza. Two more different people you won't imagine."

"The name Descartes I recognise. Spinoza no. And you will introduce me?"

"Spinoza will be here later today. He is my lens grinder, and he's bringing new lenses."

"But they are not astronomers?"

"Oh no. We would call ourselves philosophes, I guess.

"Rene wants to explore what our existence is, he seeks a logically rigorous way to explore that. A step-by-step approach to building all knowledge and truth.

"Baruch? Well, he is intrigued with nature and God, and our ethical way of living with both.

"Me, I keenly want to investigate the universe. We are three points of a triangle."

                                    Cassini's Vision

"And you meet them sometimes even here in your laboratory?"

"I have made them view my moon around Saturn. I force them to recognise what's unquestionably out there. Unexpected. Unexplainable, maybe, but verifiable. All theory must admit what actually exists there. If we debate God's world and His universe, we ought to know what that universe is."

"No, I'm satirising," he continued. "We all three enjoy each other's searchings.

"And that lens grinding? It's a hobby, though he is very competent at it."

Huygens' kitchen had prepared a portable luncheon for three, and the butler had delivered that in the late morning.

Baruch Spinoza arrived. Introductions were made, lenses were delivered, and the business essentials of his short trip had been wrapped up in an hour. Gian, Christiaan and Baruch sat to take their snacks before Spinoza had to return today to Amsterdam. However, something was amiss.

"Baruch has a traumatic week ahead," said Huygens. "His rabbinical board has called him to trial. There is a chance it may not go well."

Cassini looked to Spinoza.

Spinoza looked to Huygens.

"I trust Giovanni," said Huygens.

"I go on trial before the elders of the Amsterdam Synagogue on Sunday. For heresy."

"Heresy? Why?"

"Let me share a story. My carriage is still an hour away."

"I was born in Portugal," he started, "but the Spanish Inquisition forced us out."

His family settled in Amsterdam. Holland was more tolerant towards Jews, and his father's merchant trade flourished. Young Baruch was a fast student, receiving a wide education including full Talmudic and language and business skills, and very early he took over the family enterprise from his ailing father.

"But this is the 1600s. The world is in ferment. Holland here is a swirling community of intellectual thought. So much is there to discover."

Calvinist Protestant disputed with dissenting free-thinking opponents. Active science and philosophy tried to live together. A remnant of old Catholic scholasticism fought the new thinkers like Descartes. Into the mix, his own traditional Jewish philosophers were still debated.

"In my curiosity, I decided to take a mentorship under one Van den Enden, a widely read ex-priest. He opened my mind onto a bright sunlight, an unlimited universe of enquiry. I was introduced to authors and thinkers both ancient and new. After a while, I started publishing my views."

He paused.

"And they came to attack you?" Galilei, again. Different. But again.

"My established reputation in the town may have saved me. I'm not sure. A lot I was publishing was unorthodox, rather reckless," he admitted.

"What offended the Rabbis was that I neglected my observance of Jewish law. I ignored the customs and themes I had inherited, my own people. I changed my name in some circles to Benedict. It was on top of that community defection that my unorthodox theses became intolerable."

Baruch Benedict Spinoza departed for Amsterdam visibly anxious.

"Giovanni, what day is your return ship?"

"Scheduled Monday."

"Should we both be in Amsterdam earlier: for Sunday?"

—



Cassini's Vision

Before mid-morning Sunday, Gian, Christiaan and Borso arrived by hired coach into Amsterdam. But even then they were too late.

The early "trial" heard no arguments, took no evidence. In ten minutes, the edict had been read and the courtroom was closed. All the alert and learned of Amsterdam in a few hours knew of the judgement, and the town was in shock.

Spinoza himself they could find nowhere. He had gone into hiding, or was protected somewhere by family or friend. A half-dozen printed copies of the decree were circulating, and Gian and Christiaan were given leave and time to make written copies they might ponder on later.

The Synagogue of Amsterdam had excommunicated Spinoza. His crimes were "evil words" and "abominable heresies", not listed.

Huygens, instead of going home to family for the night, stayed in town with his guests at a room in an inn.

The edict placed on Spinoza's head a series of old curses, curses of Lucifer, curses of hellfire, curses of pestilence and misfortune and public vengeance.

They prohibited him for life from contacting any of the Jewish community for any purpose.

All commercial activity in his name was banned. His successful trading empire would be transferred to his brother.

"When the immediate panic settles," Huygens said, "I will, I must, join him and establish new bonds. My poor friend."

"I also will letter him," promised Cassini. "Spinoza is a friend and colleague in our enlightenment, and so far I don't even know him."

# Lorenna

Christiaan handed Gian a sealed and unmarked letter as the town coach neared the Amsterdam harbour.

"Here, for you," he said. "I've been holding this for days."

Borso rented a handcart for the last few hundred steps, and the Italians went aboard.

*Dear Signor Cassini,*

*It has been a very great pleasure to be afforded your company last week.*

*Indeed, your friendship and Sig. Borso's also. Your butler is a wonderful asset to you, and a skilled conversationalist. I could say, too, he is an enjoyable flirt. Enough.*

*Sig. Cassini, this thank-you letter is not any business letter. This week, you have been good to me. You acknowledged me and my work, and many men cannot! You were always gracious, respecting my views and opinions. I have to believe you also enjoyed my company.*

*My contract here, as you know, is nearing its completion. My work frightens me. May I admit that? I have never admitted it to anyone, but to you I am asking. I am well taught, but the magnitude of my responsibilities here is daunting.*

*I would hope to return to my homeland in due course. If our paths ever might cross again, I shall be totally delighted.*

*My fond regards,*

*Lorenna Martelli*


He sat in his ship's cabin reading the note again and again. Those occasional touches on his arm—on Borso's arm, too, he could now recall. Never to Christiaan though.

Were there messages in this letter? Was it just an honest but emotional gratitude note? Bother that woman! Read it again. Meanings were everywhere. Codes. Or not?


*"paths ... totally delighted."*

*"not any business letter."*

*"may I admit?"*

*"enjoyable flirt."*

*"enjoyed my company."*

*"hope to return."*

*"you I am asking."*


The ship sailed into the night. Gian did not sleep.

In the dawn, he woke Borso, and had him also read the note.

"I'm not a flirt!"

"Then I can see what you were not seeing," Gian tried to laugh.

The astronomer and his "butler"—"I'm not a butler, either!"—were on a pitching ship far from home. For the morning the two men sat on the squally deck and discussed and admitted to each other personal matters they could have not imagined. They talked of home. They talked of work.

They talked long of Celia. And above all they talked about that Lorenna.

The ship put into London.

The agreement was sealed. Borso went back to Amsterdam, and Gian sailed towards home.

—

Christiaan Huygens within the year returned Cassini's visit. He sailed around Italy to Venice.

"I have not ever been to Venice," he had messaged.

After exercising his Calvinist-attuned eyes on the willing evils of Venice, he hired two horses and a horseman to guide him to Bologna. He had been given instructions to rest the horses at the Borso-built Panzano stables if necessary. However, when he arrived, alone, at the Cassini home, the horses had earlier started back to home.

"I have a gift for you, Giovanni," he said as he came up to dinner. It was a Friday, as it chanced.

He was carrying, guardedly, a pendulum clock.

"I am proud to say I have a patent registration underway, and by last month a local clockmaker started producing these for me. This is the fifth one he made."

"Christiaan, I now have the only such clock in all Italy. For many years I tried to make Galilei's clock practical, and I couldn't. I admire you so." He took possession of his gift.

The clock mechanisms were built into a gilt box about six inches to a side. A long chain looped twice under that, with weight and pulley. And the pendulum, heavy bob on a thin rod, hung lifeless in front of the weights. For a household item, it would all be naked and vulnerable.

The weights and pendulum were easy to understand, but the magic, the mechanick's fine skills, were in the box. Celia's godlet who dealt out methodically the parcels, the ticks, of time.

Borso inspected the box, left the room and returned a moment later with tools. Within minutes, he had attached the Huygens clock to the wall. With a father's care, Huygens adjusted his baby and started the swing. And the tick.

"I hear it," said Celia.

Cassini poured each a glass of wine, and one more.

Cat walked in, brushed Borso's leg, and sat beneath the swinging pendulum, looking up.

"Cute," said the Dutchman. The cat had clean white paws and white head, but its ears and body were a light ginger.

Borso made a whistle to call Cat, but instead Cat stretched up the wall, standing on hind legs, trying to swipe the swaying bob.

"When I was a child in Amsterdam, we were taught it was too frivolous to keep an animal, and a waste of food that could have gone to God's poor."

Lorenna came to join. Her wine was waiting.

"And further, if one did keep a cat, we were taught to trim its whiskers to keep its instincts checked, to stop it being bold."

"My family thought God created all animals strictly to serve humans," said Gian. "But Cat refuses to be trained and obedient. He learns only how to gain food and attention and petting."

"No, in Genoa, a cat was for witches," Celia said. "A cat was the Devil's animal, evil, playing with its victim. But it's not true."

"Cat is my friend," said Lorenna. She reached to stroke him, and the cat stretched himself into her fingers.

"My wife," introduced Borso. "You know, of course."

"Signora, my congratulations. Your life is different since we last saw each other across Europe. There is no doubt you are looking fine and healthy."

"Meneer Huygens, good evening. I can report, and tell your father, I am enjoying the change. It's as well that the Cassini enterprises thus far are much smaller than those of your family," she said, putting one hand on her belly. "Soon I will need more than twenty-four hours each day. Unless you can make me a clock with more magic."

"I failed clock school," said Gian. Lorenna glanced at him.

Huygens smiled. "My next effort, Signora, I promise." With his glass he held up a personal toast.

"But Gian, your Galilei failed clock school too. Just a bit. His pendulum mathematics was too simple. It needed a correction."

He would make fresh and agreeable company for dinner. Bianca had now appeared with hardly a sound, and was laying out the first course of the meal. Each place had a shallow plate with pot-roasted black carrots, peeled and sweetened. The main course already sat on the table also, a high stack of cold omelettes under a lace fly cover. Bianca vanished, to be preparing a hot sweet course for a little later.

—

On the first day, Huygens was keen to discuss his research, mathematician to peer. He was making modest progress on development of new techniques he called calculus. Calculus might make trajectory predictions of the planets very much faster than old calculation modes, if he could solve its formulas. And they both knew that long time spent calculating trajectories was the bane of every astronomer.

"I am sorely in need of a colleague or two who might share in this task," he said.

The day was a frustration, because Cassini was not interested in the deep mathematics, the unpredictable leap into new theory, work with no guarantee of a workable outcome. Huygens' calculus was positing an infinite number of samplings, and infinitely small results inside each sampling. Cassini knew how to observe what was vast. He could measure it, every day. But none of his work dabbled in infinities. Infinities smelled of religious unexplainables. He

                    Cassini's Vision

didn't know how to work with this side of Huygens, who in any case claimed to barely align with his Dutch Protestantism.

Christiaan would have to work with others on this.

"The way forward is cooperation," Huygens insisted. "Remember Paris? All those intellectuals and experimenters jostling in Paris? In this exciting time when so much science is unfolding, we must share what we know. We must make an effective network."

"Look at what we have now," he continued, "what we call our Republique des Lettres. With our writings, we are trying to make a community of philosophes across the world, even to the Americas. Nowhere do we exist in the physical, we are invisible. It's time to be looking to better ways to share our experiments. Europe needs a big Academy.

"And then we have this young fellow who is two months ago appointed as Professor of Astronomy in London. Wren. Christopher Wren. Another colleague. He will go far. We should be sharing more."

Cassini steered day two back onto moons, and Saturn's moon, Luna Saturni. He took his guest to the Panzano Observatory, an enjoyable long stroll, and they would return on the morrow. Malvasia once again had the latest telescope at Bologna.

The astrology emphasis of the Villa's business was not to the taste of Huygens, and the Marquis, who started genial, later wandered off to other tasks.

The two retired to the Observatory roof. Saturn would not be in the sky tonight, so they took turns observing several other sky bodies that were their current interests. They found two of Galilei's moons around Jupiter.

"You have been looking at my moon though?"

"Countless times. I haven't been giving it intensive observation. You will at the appropriate time publish all your observations and theories, I have presumed."

"Oh, it's coming!"

Pause.

"Gian, what's past Saturn?"

"Saturn? Nothing's past Saturn. We'd have seen it. Except comets."

"Well, what do you think is on these planets and all these moons we do see?"

"What's on them? We can't know that. I can see markings on our own Moon that look like mountains, perhaps rivers. All else is too far to see so much yet."

"I have seen some dark spots on Mars."

"What do you make them out to be?"

"I was wondering if they might be water. Or ice."

"Water?"

"On those other planets I think one day we will find living things."

"Oh?"

"Perhaps a moss or a mushroom. Does Mars have Mars mosquitoes? Or green smelly water, if that is a living thing? Or trees that are pink?"

"A dog?"

"Who knows?" said Huygens. "We have many different animals on Earth, even so many variants of dog. The Saturn dogs might be different again."

"People?"

"No," scoffed Huygens. "God created His people on Earth."

"God's people?"

It wasn't a Friday social dinner, and no Jesuit was present.

"Christiaan, tell me what you think, you. Yourself."

"I don't know." He stopped. A droll smile grew.

"We need vision," he said.

"If those planets, or those moons, had water, there might be life there. Water might make it all possible. Liquid water."

"Dark, you said. Black water?"

"Possibly it's ice water? So far from the Sun it must be colder. But on other planets the water might be different water, to avoid freezing. Maybe our Earth type water would boil on Venus, and then perhaps their own Venus water does not."

"Perhaps, perhaps! Tell me, as a scientist, how can you demonstrate this planet life? In our lifetime? Planning to pay a visit?"

"You and me, we are born too early."

"And we are born with overlords in fine robes who define what we are allowed to see and know."

"Only for you in Bologna. I no longer give them such a right. You do choose to live in the most Papal city outside Rome."

"Well tomorrow, we will enjoy what this problematic Bologna offers. The following day I will introduce you to my mentor the Jesuit Battista." His shield. The advocate. Huygens was more right than Gian wanted to admit.

—

On his departure after five days, Huygens again offered his reflections on his once financial advisor.

"That woman is a mystery. What I see here bears little resemblance to the Lorenna Martelli we employed. Here she radiates contentment. I can see she wants to be family mother. And yet, and yet ... and yet still she is the one who organises, is in control, keeps all things in order. The planner, the administrator. I am impressed, and I shall tell my father we never understood who she was."

No, they had not.

"We love our Renna," said Gian.

"Does Celia ever get concerned that Lorenna drives her household staff? Your capable Bianca and the other two girls, and the maintenance and gardens man?"

Gian laughed. "You misjudge Celia. She gets relieved of chores she finds boring. My Celia is happy being artist primadonna.

"Celia owns the place, and Lorenna runs it."

Again he laughed.

"Well, your household functions well. Lorenna keeps you to an efficient family enterprise. Upright. Pious. Very moral."

Lorenna had arranged that two horses had been fetched from Panzano stable, and the two men prepared to leave for Genoa harbour.

It was indeed, mused Gian, becoming a flourishing family business. His stipend was generous, and Celia's gallery was profitable and growing in prestige. Old Uncle Antonio's contacts and Lorenna's instincts had made a wise foundation for the Cassini household investments.

She did indeed, mused Huygens, run a flourishing business for that family. He had watched the young Lorenna so homesick in The Hague, had seen her Italian eyes light up when Borso was around. Why don't you find a devious way to send Borso a message, he had hinted.

—

Lorenna was leaning aside, nursing her baby. Friday dinners were her highlight.

They were all eating in the main floor sala, beneath the fine private selection of Celia's paintings from the Bologna women's studio. Celia had kept these aside—they were not on show to any clients.

Battista did not always take for granted the largesse of his Friday hosts. In his trade of being a professional cleric, he had cleric colleagues, more cloistered and less secular than he, who grew the grapes and made the wine needed for Holy Mass. Battista was a most persuasive bargainer, and as a result the Cassini family wine stocks were on occasional Fridays very substantially refilled.

Gian Cassini understood their unspoken pact, its layers, but he enjoyed Battista's company and the mood he brought to the other guests of many Friday dinners.

"Crete? Both Renna and I have been in Crete," said Borso.

"True?" Battista said, turning.

"Yes, I was about eight," she said.

"Crete is a dangerous place. Under siege for years. I understood you were a Venice child."

"Tell him your story, Renna," said Gian. "The Crete story. The Father has never heard it."

Lorenna hesitated, then handed Gian the baby, and Cassini cradled the infant, peered into its sleepy face, and smiled.

She sat at the table.

"Father Tista, I did grow up in Venice. Many of my play years I spent frightening my mother by hanging around the lost and hidden waterways. Some years it had been too hard to play. Some years had no playmates.

"My family has been an old merchant dynasty for three hundred years. We used to be very rich, but it's tougher now. Venice lost more than half its population in the last plagues. The Doge died, lots of our family died, and the military and the town officials and our seamen, they all died. Those left had to put back together what we had."

"But Lorenna dear," said Gian, "it was not only Venice that fell into such darkness and turmoil. The soldiers of the War brought the Death to Milan, too."

Celia glanced up from her eating. "It seems that the trading ports in particular attracted the pestilence, because I too have memories of the mighty fear and horror in my own Genoa."

Lorenna pressed on. "Venice as a capital of a merchant empire has for many years suffered attacks from the Ottoman Turks. For a long time the Turks have wanted our trade. Within our weakened family business, the company posted my father to Crete."

"But why Crete?"

"Crete sits astride the Dardanelles, and is strategic in monitoring shipping between Constantinople and all Europe, Venice included. I was a child, so I understood little of the deadly politics and jealous military manoeuvring that was afoot.

"But it was a marvellous adventure to be in another country. I used to sit near the port where the pirate boats from Malta came in. They offloaded the goods they stole from Ottoman merchant ships. The Maltese Knights considered it God's correct work to humiliate the Turks."

"The Turks are heathens!" said the priest.

"But they are not heathen," said Gian. "They may be mistaken on the name and the nature of God, but they do still fight for a god I approximately recognise. The heathen have no God at all."

"The Maltese buccaneers had called them people of the Devil," she said. "The relentless Maltese campaign was quite unfortunate for us. As we owned Crete, the Turks concluded the pirates were in league with us. Therefore, we were now the enemy rather than trading colleagues. The Turkish warships laid siege to Crete's port cities, a siege still existing. We starved. My family were smuggled out after about six months."

"Lorenna, my child, I had no idea you had such adventures. Where did you learn your undoubted abilities in business and finance that mark your life now in Cassini's household?"

Lorenna paused.

"Come on," pleaded the jovial and well-fed guest, "you must share with us."

She looked at Borso, but did not catch his attention. She glanced to Giovanni. Gian was looking at the baby, absorbed.

                    Cassini's Vision

"No, not today. I'll just say that my family was a merchant company. We understood the world of trading and shipping and finance. And more. Those are the skills I was taught. We all were."

"Gian," she confided after the priest had gone, "he pushes me for more. It's too tangled."

—

"Lorenna, I loved your stories of your growing up," said the priest on the following Friday. "Today, please, you must tell us more. Enthral us. Why was your family sent to Crete?"

Oh, dear.

"But first, Father, would you bless my new beads for me?"

He crossed them briefly and mumbled a prayer.

"We grew cotton in Crete, Father Tista. My father was appointed supervisor for the several plantations our family operated on Crete. Venice no longer has easy access to the lands further East, because, as I said, the Ottoman are now firmly positioned across all the ports and routes leading East. For the past two hundred years we have been growing crops closer to home, on Cypress while we held that, and on Crete. Crete has very fertile high plateaus, and my family owned extensive estates."

"All cotton?"

"Earlier we cropped sugar, shipping as always through Venice to the rest of Europe. But the sugar business collapsed because of the new Spanish and Portuguese imports from the New World across the Atlantic. We had been too successful growing sugar, and our methods have been used as models for the Brazil and West Indies sugar trades.

"On sugar, we no longer competed, but we still were cropping cotton. It was these Mediterranean crops my family has specialised in for two centuries, the growing and the shipping and the trading into Europe."

"The sugar trade of the Brasilieros is serviced by slave labour."

She jolted. The lashings, the languages, the arbitrary evil fortune of those abducted, the diseases, the chains, the screams and the smell of death and fear.

"... by slave labour," he was saying. "Is that why you could not compete?"

"Our Crete and Cypress plantations were operated by slaves also, from before the New World slaves. Bulgarians worked for us as slaves, and Tartars and Turks, not African blacks as in the Caribbean. Between us and the Turks, slave taking happened both ways along the Mediterranean.

"So, you see, cotton is the story of why I was in Crete. We ran plantations.

"The other half of the family was involved in the shipbuilding, carpentry and sailmaking back in Venice itself, but that's not my story."

And she would not reveal, either, how much more money was made from the slaves than the cotton.

Stop, stop.

"But your story does include travelling to the Dutch Republic. Borso first met you at The Hague, I heard."

"For twelve months I was assigned to work at the house of Huygens in Amsterdam. I met Borso when he and Gian were there three years ago."

The priest was relentless. "Holland has no plantations. Holland has its own Empire."

"Of course there are no plantations. Remember that my training is in money and business dealings. My family had serious and awkward debts to the Huygens family from some trade contracts. As payment, I was indentured to work as an administrator to Huygens."

"That sounds to me like you were a slave."



Cassini's Vision

"No, I was not! In that house, I had honour and freedom. My work was respected and valuable. Holland is the most sophisticated commerce and investment culture in the world. They think big and they plan long. I restructured the finances of the Huygens assets, and I returned to Italy with favourable references and goodwill. I paid out my family debt."

"Still it appears to me as though they sent you on a mission of service. If it was not slavery, it was still demeaning for a young professional woman. You occupied all that time when any young woman should have been snaring a regular and respected husband."

Did the priest realise the slight he was making? Borso was a hard worker. "I have a husband who suits me well."

Pause.

"I have what I deserve. Better."

No, unwise.

"Oh dear, excuse my clumsiness, yes, yes, you are well matched."

She paused again, then buried her face in her hands.

When she looked up, Cat had jumped onto the table. She brushed it off.

Damn this man. She straightened her shoulders, sat tall.

"Father, I am about to confess to you, and to my family here, some things that have shamed me to near despair. You are a man of the Lord who has known the foibles of many, and I shall be surprised if you think too badly of me.

"After my family escaped to Venice from Crete, and when I was about fourteen, I had a problem with an old uncle in our family, a man of feeble temperament. Let me say that I was despoiled by this man.

"I was terrified. The family discovered what had happened, and they contained the scandal as best they could. If I were not willingly evil, then I was still marked forever as at least a damaged young woman with limited marriage prospects. I was worth money as a worker for the family, but I was likely not marriageable.

"I had lived with that sentence for the years before Borso arrived in Venice to ask for me."

Before Cassini sent Borso back to ask for her.

"That was more than I had expected to be my lot." She fought her tears. "Only during my year in Holland, what you call my servitude, did I feel unwatched and untainted. That's why I said my life now is even better than I believed I could have asked for." Celia moved to her side and put an arm around her.

Battista stopped. Embarrassed finally, he protested his apology and made to depart.

—

The next morning, Lorenna walked to the convent. Cassini and Borso were inspecting a new telescope today. Celia was home with the children; her art collective did not meet on Saturdays. Lorenna pulled on the bell chain at the door.

After a wait, the beams unbolted, the door creaked open, and young Sister ArcAngel appeared.

"Signora Lorenna, good morning, I will find Mother for you. Come inside to the parlour, please." This was the formality. Lorenna was always allowed into the convent, its common room and its chapel: she spent many hours there sewing and talking with the nuns. The discussion was a mix of pious gentility and earthly banter.

She would come often on the afternoons of painting. One woman from the art community would visit the convent to give guidance to the would-be painters. Not many of these nuns had real talent, but all were obliged to attend and to try or pretend.

Lorenna enjoyed that painting, the glorious mess of easels and brushes and cloths, although she knew she could never have the artistic instincts Celia had. Celia never saw her here, hence there was never an occasion she would be judged or compared.

Many times, Lorenna would come to the convent to be in the chapel. It was a private chapel, but Lorenna was welcomed. She could sit opposite the nuns, still sharing their ceremonies, trying always to believe.

Today, she just wanted to sit alone. Mother Superior led her to a chapel seat and left.

My God, oh my God, I live among happiness more than I thought I had earned. But sometimes my soul is so tormented.

Why?

Why?

When one day my whole life is weighed, I wish I be not found wanting. I wish when I die my sins can be washed away. My God, in the state of Your holy grace I want to be worthy to enter the Heaven of the righteous.

# Bologna

It was a Wednesday in the early afternoon when the priest Riccioli arrived again at the Cassini home. Only the women and two of the children were home, but Celia was busy painting.

Lorenna was puzzled.

"Lorenna, I need a friend. I need to talk. Can you spare me some time?"

"Father, always you can have the time. Come in."

The Jesuit could be difficult, but he was not a threat.

"Thank you. My soul is unhappy, and I would like to talk where I can trust someone will listen."

"A drink?"

"No wine, please. Clarity demands no wine."

This wasn't the usual Battista.

They walked in the garden. He stayed only ten minutes. He asked no advice; he asked just for a friend's ear, even a woman's.

What had set loose this inner courage? It must have been her openness in baring her own soul a week earlier.

"These are the demons within me," he finished. "Thoughts that can never agree with the teachings and training I have been believing for years. Pray for me." With that, he was gone.

She went up to the door outside her bedroom. A tiny shelf there in the corridor held a small lamp—a bowl of oil and a floating wick. The housemaid lit one lamp on each floor at early evening.

But beside the night-lamp, Lorenna had persuaded Borso to install another compact shelf, an altar, with a miniature of the Virgin Mary on the wall. The Mary icon was a birthday gift from Celia, by Celia, last year.

Lorenna lit the lamp, and moved it to the Mary altar. It might ward off anything that was not comfortable.

Now she was comfortable.

—

"Celia, I intend going to London. I want to meet my counterpart there, one Christopher Wren. He holds the Professorship of Astronomy at London, operating out of Gresham College."

"Is it time we went abroad, you and I, as a respectable and respected couple? Taking grand carriages on the historic streets of London? Seeing the sights, trying new foods, practising some English?"

She blanched. "By ship?"

"Yes, in a month or so."

Gian had planned for some time how to broach this request. How to make it sound attractive. How to jump past her reticence. How to explore with his wife what else might be out there.

But it all fell flat, and so he prepared to sail alone.

He had ample time aboard, after recovering from his now expected seasickness, to read the inaugural address of Wren on the day he had taken up the astronomy position. Ironically, it was written in Latin, but to an Italian, Latin was easy fare.

*I take this task with humility and gratitude. I am I know still a young man, and the task is large.*

How were the English with such little effort holding together both Copernicus and God? "Working together"? In Italy one could be tortured.

Gian was looking forward to this encounter.

He disembarked at Southampton.

Sometimes, however, history has its own disruptive agenda. Something was wrong in this England of 1658, very wrong.

Hailing a carriage, he requested Gresham College.

"Ah, Mister, you don't want to be going to Gresham, I think. Gresham is a soldier barracks this last fortnight, and they's wrecking the place so fast."

"Very well, but take me to look."

Doors were burnt, the whole area smelled of excrement, and ill-dressed soldiers and others came and went.

Gian now had no plan.

"They's all been sent away," the driver volunteered. "Shall we go there?"

Cassini was let off at a small stone house a mile hence, and he paid his driver.

"Oh, yes, Professor Cassini, quite, yes, of course. John-Dominic, welcome to our London." Wren was a short and slight man, and yes, young.

Oliver Cromwell, he who had earlier executed King Charles and waged civil wars, had died. The stalemated political tensions of England had snapped again. Cromwell's ineffective brother Richard and other contenders were now battling for control of the country. Protestant against Catholic, royalist against parliament. Family against family. Intrigue versus plot. Social and constitutional chaos.

No one was winning, no one had a strong plan. But people were dying.

Cassini sought the first available ship out of Southampton.

"My dear Christiaan," he wrote, back on ship. He would put mail ashore at Marseilles. "I have just walked into a hell."

*I visited our colleague Mister Wren. He is not at Gresham College because that place is now a barracks for civil war. But I must believe you in Holland know by now the news of England's crisis. On my ship's journey from Italy I had suspected nothing until I came ashore.*

*Christiaan, it is difficult to imagine that England, so industrious, so fine in its philosophy and its research, can for a very long time recover from what chaos I saw. It can no longer be a powerful or influential nation in this growing world, I fear. It's lost its soul. I was scared I might lose my own soul there. But then a soul is not something you believe in anyway; we have argued that before today.*

*In my short stay, I was still pleased to have at least some fruitful discussions with Wren. Besides his astronomy work and the classes he teaches on that subject, well attended and regarded I might add, he has weekly gatherings at Gresham. No, he used to have them, with a motley group of thinkers and secular intellectuals. Some were experimenters and some were philosophers only. It was some of those gentlemen whom I found hidden with him in a small house in London.*

*Two things left strong impression on me in my very brief visit.*

*Firstly, it was clear that Wren's regular philosophe group was planning or hoping to incorporate into a permanent London academy of learning and discovery. This news should be joy to your heart. But for now, England is in such trauma, having neither a king nor a working parliament, there can be no way of Wren's academy group being granted patronage or endorsement. They must wait for more stable politics first.*

*The second excitement I had in London was to discuss with Wren our common work on seeing the planets and the heavens. His telescope was unworkable, stored in a back room of his safety house. But we spoke through the night on subjects dear to both our souls. That word souls again!*

*I do understand ever more plainly why you believe we need to share with our colleagues what we know and what we find.*

*Yours,*

*Giovanni Cassini*

—

Celia's cherished studiola, her own retiring space with desk and bed and books, had long ago moved upstairs into the Cassini storey. Room had been needed down near the kitchen for the resident kitchen maid and the housemaid who had joined Bianca on the staff. But Celia still had her botega, her work studio, on the ground floor not far from the portego gallery. She painted sometimes at home, and sometimes at the painting academy.

Gian when entertaining a formal colleague always used the lounging hall or the sala dining room on the principal *piano nobile* storey. Bianca's mastery of her kitchen and her assistants had grown to match the standard of food and presentation befitting a middle-ranking Bologna professor.

Celia, on the other hand, had in the past few years hosted three banquets for her art community and prospective clients. These she arranged downstairs in the portego, where each time she prepared and hung a careful selection of her works.

For the first banquet, she contracted in a team of a French chef and his crew of four. Bianca stood aside, as she had agreed years before.

The foreign chef had helped Celia outfit her servery with plates, trays and pitchers of new tin-glazed ceramic featuring colourful pictures and emblems. This majolica ceramic ware had become a much-admired product, and it drew attention every time it was brought out.

Celia hired the chef only once, and Bianca was restored to full mistress of her kitchen. Celia admitted her skills: Bianca could deliver dinner service befitting an artist having recognition and a comfortable market.

—

"Oh, here you are, Celi," Gian said, "This Friday I have invited a friend you have never met, I believe. You may know his name. It's Salvator Rosa."

Celia was on a ladder hanging a fresh work on the portego wall. "I need this one positioned to sweep the eye through onto our garden," she mumbled.

"Where is your assistant?"

Celia employed a helper on three mornings each week.

"Her father is quite ill. I gave her leave for a week, and it might be longer."

"Then you should let me send Borso to do that."

The artist paused. She turned her body and then her head. A small ball of sticky wax was between her teeth, held dry, wax to steady the painting from swaying. She took the wax from her teeth.

"Rosa? Rosa! The Roman rebel?"

"The same. I was privileged to have his company and his wisdom many years ago in Florence. I was but a youth, and he adopted me—for only one day mind you—into the secrets and the intrigues of the art world there."

"Salvator Rosa? Your friend? I thought you were an engineer, an astronomer?"

"The University pays me as a mathematician."

"I don't care. No one thinks of you as an artist. That's my job. Rosa from Rome!"

"Well, this week he's not in Rome. He was at a function today on the campus, and I re-introduced myself. He remembered our day in Florence well. I invited him here, and he accepted at once."

"For you? Or for me?"

"For the enlightenment of us both," he said.

"You're being pompous!"

"I think he wants to track how I got from then to here. He said also that he knows well of your reputation, as Bellini. I'm sure you can have a lot of fun with this fellow."

"I want the portego, I want the gallery," she cried. "We'll do banquet style, but just the few of us. A Friday. Yes."

Definitely it would be the Bellini Gallery. A mind meeting of opinionated artists. Where else?

—

"Borso, you stand across here with that sword high and ready, because I'm coming for you, they're coming for you," Sal said.

You can't call me Rosa or Salvator, he had started, I'm Sal.

"They're coming over the rail. A dozen of them, clambering," Borso screamed. For an hour they had stormed around their "stage", Sal directing.



Cassini's Vision

"They're off-balance at this moment. Chop off one hand, or strike the head. Let them fall back onto each other. You are in possession of the deck. Hold your ship. Desperate and ferocious. But STOP."

All the actors stopped in a frozen pose.

Sal dropped his voice.

"Celia, some caution. Caution mixed with your horror. You should peer around the cabin. That musket you wield, you are not sure if you have loaded it correctly, but it's your only weapon. Let's push that chest ... here ... that can be the cabin corner. Now, again, you are terrified." His pitch rose. "Mess your hair more. Good. You get one shot if the musket works. In that turmoil over the rail," and he now yelled, "pick your mark. You will be the key to the battle."

"No, stop," said Sal, "again. Celia, swap with Renna. Renna holds the musket." They swapped.

When the scene was set, the moment frozen, Sal called Celia to walk around and view from every angle.

"In your mind's eye, what else can you see. The raging sea? Others quivering in the background? What background? Perhaps the captain's hat slips, distracting him? Others are boarding on the other side? Is anyone else coming to help? Bodies or moaning marauders on the deck? What will we make the centre of this drama, the focus of interest? And when we paint it, what angle, what lighting, what structure on the canvas?

"And then stop again. Think. It's a sea battle with boarding pirates. When was this? Last year? Battle of Lepanto like your piece on the wall over there? Romans versus Phoenicians? Troy?"

"Except for the musket, it could be any," replied Celia, her breath ragged.

She had thrown off her wig. Her real hair straggled across her face. The makeup was smeared, and her brow black ran.

"Then what excites you? You are the painter. It's a human drama in any century. Which do you want to paint?"

Celia hesitated.

For three hours in the early afternoon, the beauty madam had visited, and had applied her mixtures of lemon, borax and egg, and then a ground pearl powder, to whiten Celia's face, and some mercury-based cinnabar for the red. Black paint had shaped the eyebrows. It was a beauty indulgence Celia had used rarely.

All destroyed. This intense drama had not been planned.

"Celia, which battle would you have a client want to buy, if you painted it to hang in your gallery? Does your buyer want a scene of celebration or of horror and destruction?"

"Hmm, something epic Greek, or a Genoa or Venice sea battle."

She continued, "But my clients are more today from France or further into Europe, and agents buy for them."

"And from that, what will you paint? To your passion or to your market? For the love of your paints, or for the feel of the money?"

Again she had no reply.

"Because it's my own opinion," he whispered, "that when you paint for the money, you will see less money over time."

Celia stayed silent.

Cassini went to the sideboard, saved from the shipboard raid, and poured five glasses of a pink wine.

"That's it?" asked Borso. "We don't fight on?"

They all sat. Dinner was still forty minutes away. Bianca's team had been working since yesterday to deliver a classy mini-banquet for five.

"No, we think on the drama. We try to see its history and its meaning."

"A fight is a fight. My ship was boarded and taken captive. It was a real fight."

"How many died?"

"No one died. We surrendered."

"That's drama?"

"I was taken as a slave. That's drama!"

"Agreed. That's drama. Could make excellent canvas material."

Celia retired a while to salvage her face.

Cassini and Salvator went into the garden to walk and talk, to re-connect to an earlier time.

The others disbanded, to meet again in time for the dinner.

—

Bianca rang her hand bell in the kitchen. Dinner would be ready in fifteen minutes. On time.

Lorenna and Borso came down. The two men emerged from the courtyard. They gathered, standing, at one end of the portego, looking into the garden.

Celia stormed back down. "How did you know? How did you know what I'm thinking?"

"I don't know what you think," said Salvator.

"The money versus my passion. My ideals. The realities I keep searching for. The yearning of my youth. I am seduced by the wealth."

Her face still sweated and glowed through the makeup.

"I despise I am being seduced. I must retain my scepticism. See what we have in this life, this Italy, this Bologna, this Earth, this political and religious turmoil. Where are the other ways to live, other facts to find? I know they must exist. Too many things are wrong with this world we are living in."

Tears filled her eyes.

Gian scratched his head.

Lorenna thumped the sideboard with her fist. Her red wig—her only attempt at dressing up—was still on.

"No, Celi," said Lorenna, "what you say is not right. This world is our testing ground. We are here to enjoy it and to love it, to do our best in it. Some things on this Earth and in Heaven we will never understand. But they are our world nevertheless. We must believe in it, trust in what we have.

"If we don't believe in the world we see, then we have nothing left, we cannot be functional people. We can't be people without having beliefs in this world. We should stop trying always to change everything, stop looking too far beyond what we have and see."

"Would it matter what we believe? Or is it sufficient we believe in just something? Anything?" asked Sal.

"Perhaps we just need things to believe, anything to believe. It makes us secure. Then we can live as humans. I don't know." Lorenna started to cry. "I grew up with too much adventure and change. It hasn't nourished my soul."

Bianca's two girls, in uniform, came in and offered sweet treats, and a short glass of a spirit. Salvator cocked his face Gian's way as a question.

"I don't know what it's called. Our gardener handyman makes his own, from New World maize. Bianca scores some for us on occasions. Try it."

The spirit starter brought calm.

Gian brought them all to table.

"Act Three," suggested Sal.

The Murano chandelier was alight above them. A cold soup awaited each at their place. A pig's head had been placed mid table, surrounded by piles of pre-carved pork. Sauces, breads, vegetables and three wines were all set out. With the soup they began their feast, and the maids at the same time served all their first main plate.

Gian said, "Sal, I've brought you up-to-date on my story, our story, Genoa, my illicit visit upon old Galileo in Florence while you were there in exile. About the astronomy for the astrology master, the Count. And how we came to live in Bologna as city astronomer and mathematician.

"I'll leave Celia to spin her own tale later, but now it's time you tell us your story. Entertain us. Go back to the start."

"Yes," said Borso, "why were you in exile?"

"Hah, that's near the end of my story. My life has had too many chapters.

"I was low-born. I learned my painting in the Naples school. Back then I was a brooding romantic. My landscapes were full of ruin and melancholy and rebellion. Calm and idyllic scenes were not my interest.

"When I was twenty-three I moved to Rome, and I wrote and painted and etched and acted in theatre."

"Ah," said Borso.

"I wrote an amount of satirical comment, stirring the Roman politics as though it were a kitchen pot. My sarcasm offended Bernini, a Roman sculptor with plenty of influence. Answer to your earlier question, Borso: I took myself to Florence. As Rome had been, Florence was an art community with another set of skills and expectations, and so being the rebel was a natural there.

"In Florence, I got some cover from a Medici Cardinal who loved my heathenism. I painted little, but I founded the salon of varied artists, a lot of poets and playwrights."

"The *Academy of the Stricken*," said Gian. "I went there!"

"When it became safe, I returned to Rome, where I could paint monstrous canvases of death and carnage and burning and pagan witches and mighty moments in history. Big drama."

"We know you like drama. When the Turks sailed me in chains to Constantinople, does that make a worthy canvas?"

"Was your arm hanging on by a thread, and everything burning around you down to the waterline, and Lucifer cackling as you stumbled and slipped in your own blood?"

"No. But I smoked hemp in the deserts in the Moghul Empire. Is that drama? I abducted a woman from the Netherlands to smuggle her to Italy."

Lorenna grinned.

"Sal," said Borso, "tell me more drama."

"I fought in a nine-day war in Naples more than ten years ago. We went to war against Spain who own Naples. A smuggler called Masaniello from Amalfi led us into war to stop the Spanish taxing us into penury. In secret, we recruited an army of a thousand assassins from among the street urchins. We ransacked the armoury and opened the gaols. The Spanish Viceroy surrendered and Masaniello negotiated a new charter for Naples."

"Yes. That makes drama," said Celia.

"The treaty lasted a few months. Then they murdered the fellow."

"You've painted all that?"

"So many ways. Even Masaniello's portrait."

Celia's eyes were far away. "A wild artist," she murmured.

"Are you happy now, Sal?" asked Lorenna. "Your life, I mean," recognising the ambiguity.

"Happy is not the question. I'm very alert. Many take a dark view of my satires and topics. I poke fun at those I need to live among. In my savage tale of Babylon, everyone knew I referenced Rome. My tongue I fear is too clever by half."

"Tell."

"Of course. One painting I called *Allegory of Fortune* was taken by many to mean that some artists got overpaid for mediocre talent. The result? A lot of that mediocre talent came after my blood."

"Did you mean to imply that?"

"Oh yes! And then the witch canvases had the Inquisition fellows asking rather too many dangerous questions."

"Your life is all jolly. All adventure and risk." Celia shook her head. Admiration. Astonishment. A lust of her soul.

"Only maybe," he said after a pause. "My son and my brother died when the plague came through Naples last year."

He paused another moment.

"My boy was not legitimate; he was the child of my dear mistress Lucrezia. So even my son's death I could not grieve openly. Not all is levity, Celia."

No one spoke for a while.

Every tide comes in, and then goes out.

Ignore the money, decided Celia. Paint my life and my passions. Magic and its courage. Forward to the unknown. Lorenna's way is not my way.

There has to be, decided Borso, a drama canvas in my weeks walking the desert tied to a camel. Talk to Celi.

I still have hope, decided Giovanni, if this rebel in Rome itself can survive the Inquisition.

Lorenna decided. She went to the garden to peer back inwards to the portego. Must talk with the gardener: major work is overdue. But the budget is healthy.

—

Celia headed down for breakfast. The children had gone down already, and the baby was sleeping.

The Cassinis' quarters were the top storey, and the family there included by now the young adults Lucia and Piero, wishing soon to be away on their own lives. They had too the boy Andro, anguishing and edgy in puberty. The last was the colicky infant Carla, the unexpected one. Celia had lost one child, but four left was a respectable family.

Celia came off the stairs into the living space storey beneath the Cassinis. She was grumpy. And hungry. She was late, but food should still be available.

The others were eating. The bread was hot from the oven.

"Academy, academy, schemademy, phukademy, cyclademy," she said. "Everyone wants to start an academy. Academies of Art and Literature and Philosophy."

"I don't want to start an academy," replied Lorenna. "And I wish you'd not be obscene when the kids are around. Already here I have an academy for infant feeding, child taming, and food planning in between." She was running a busy household, and all the finances, and thriving at it.

"Gian, there's another request here from Florence. Would you join the Leopoldo de Medici's Academy of Experimentation? His *Accademia del Cimento*? Lorenna threw the invite out, but I rescued it."

Lorenna frowned.

"Test and test again, they want. Measure everything and obtain real facts. Build your science on testing, and not on an ancient Greek parchment." Celia was skimming it.

"Hey," said Borso, "give the boss some credit. Everything he does is testing, testing, observing and recording."

"He's right, Celi, everything I do now is documenting observed facts. Besides, being in a court patronage is a risk to the true science. The academy member can become beholden to the money source and the influence peddlers. But Florence? My old friend sold his soul to the de Medicis there; he became an emblem of royal power. When he needed help badly, they couldn't protect him. No thanks. They asked me earlier, a few years ago, and I said no then. It's still no."

Gian finished his breakfast.

"And besides, Leopold's academy is a rehash of Galilei's school. The people are Galilei's old students. The aim is again prestige to the court."

He glanced to Borso.

"No. Our work will stand by itself."

The men departed for the day. The youngsters wandered away.

"Renna, sorry, yes, I should have left it in the throwaway pile. He knows where he's going. That's why we love him so."

They finished eating, not ready yet to go off to their tasks. The maid cleared away.

"You happy to have my girl today?" Most days Lorenna could absorb her into her own brood. Slept her, changed her, nursed her.

"Sure, always, I love the kids."

"Lorenna, when you worked in Holland, your job was important, wasn't it?"

"It was. I was only twenty, Celi."

"And Borso persuaded you to come here and be family with him?"

She knew, they both knew, the story was different then, but the repeated public version somehow became its own truth after a while.

"I've always found it puzzling that you left that intoxicating work in a new land, and made a more domestic life back here."

"Do I look happy?"

"You appear motherly, cheerfully, smilingly, healthily happy."

"That's my answer," Lorenna said, barely audible. "I'm a lover."

"Funny." Celia spoke softly too. "I had thought I was 'the lover'."

"But you are. A different lover. The hard-skinned one. The one who got the earlier start. Are we okay?"

"Lorenna, we've always been correct."

"But we hide."

# The Stakes

It was her art collective morning. But Celia had taken herself instead to the offices of Fr Riccioli.

"Celia my dear, what a surprise. Please come to my humble abode."

Humble it was not.

"The man is feeling well? He was poorly the last I saw him on Thursday. I hope it was a fleeting illness."

"Giovanni is fine, Father. I come for myself."

"Sit down, sit down." The armed chairs were broad and luxuriant. "I'll call for drinks."

She waited. She collected her wits, dampened her anger.

He returned carrying two cool lemon waters.

He's organised that himself, she thought.

"Father, I have a problem."

"A priest listens to every problem." He smiled.

"This problem includes you, Father." The smile went.

"Father Tista, I am sure you mean no harm, but some of your remarks in our household, and I insist we love having you, some of your quips are causing anxiety in our home."

"Oh dear, I'm so sorry. What am I doing so out of order?"

"It's a single issue, Father. It's about my son Andro."

"Ah, young curly."

"Please stop. It's exactly that. He is a curly top kid. I want you not to mention that. We don't want him imagining himself different among us."

"You don't want to hear me calling him curly?"

"In particular, we don't want him hearing you call him out as different. It hurts us all. That's all."

"No, it's not all," she continued. "I want you to not think on it yourself, Father."

Celia departed distressed for her family. Yes, it was all her family. This was the family she had built. This priest, friend or no, was not going to break it.

She would give Riccioli one credit: she had never seen him accept like all other Roman clerics anyone touching his shoes or his cassock in superstitious fawning.

—

Lorenna the household administrator, with Borso the "boss's" technical assistant, occupied the first storey up from the ground. This was the mezzanine in the comfortable Bologna Cassini home. From the time of her arrival, Lorenna had always had her own room, and they had also a child room, and a guest room that the nursemaid used now. Their premises were complete enough that if they wished they could live their private hours secluded as any married couple with two youngsters might cherish. They could even cook a little, and wash and sleep in their separate world if they chose.

Today, however, Lorenna was resting upstairs, as often they all did. Celia's Carla was finally asleep, in the care of the maid.

The best storey of the house, the finest furnished and decorated, the level with the grandest windows, was one storey above the mezzanine. Perhaps the builder had intended this *piano nobile* storey as only for dining in the sala at one end and formal entertainment in the hall, or business meeting space. However, in practice, the two families, one above, one below, used it for most of their leisured living. The house staff were accustomed to quick cleanup and conversion for formal activities.

Lorenna slumped into a low soft chair in the broad main floor. She knew it would be a problem when she wanted to stand again. She was heavy with her third child, and it was warm today. When the wind came from the wrong quarter, little breeze came through the house.

Today, bumps and intermittent scraping noises came down through the house. Borso had been all day upstairs with the builders.

Cassini had been grumbling to Borso a month ago about the awkward operation of his telescope on the roof. By next morning Borso presented him with design sketches for a windowed dome to cover the telescope.

Today the builders had started installing the new roof dome. Gian's telescope and its associated equipment were shifted aside undercover and out of the weather and dust. The first day's work was mainly demolition.

The new dome for the small Campani instrument was to rest on a huge circular wooden ring. One person, with effort, would be able to rotate the dome. A narrow unglazed window would run down one side of this dome.

To support this rotatable dome, they were to construct the telescope base into the floor.

This sort of mechanical task and supervision suited Borso.

Lorenna had so learned in time to love him with a great tenderness. That they were both game pieces in a grander play she had long accepted.

It was Gian she had snared successfully those years ago. She had only a single opportunity to do that, one chance, and she had won. That astonishing and clever man-god, and Italian, the unexpected one, who breezed into her faraway, stressed and unsustainable world.

                    Cassini's Vision

Gian came with a price. Everything of high value comes with a heavy price in this life. It was God's just balance.

She knew it was out of order to bid for him. It was utterly outrageous.

I was desperate. I hated Amsterdam.

Borso had sailed back to Holland with Cassini's proposition. Lorenna had agreed.

In his world, Gian had insisted to her the deal was not wrong. Convincing her it wasn't wrong was not easy: he was a man.

Lorenna knew it was also unreasonable to Celia that she had asked for Gian.

Then she quickly learned she was mistaken again.

And after a time she believed it was never wrong all along, even for her. It just needed courage and love. It did not deserve scruples.

There was no price.

I should have known better. I'm a Venice woman.

Her baby moved.

Lorenna had never used a balia for her two, but nursed them herself. She by now had weaned those two, but instead was now nursing Celia's Carla. She would run her fingers through the baby's curly hair and contemplate the meanings and the complications of love.

When she assembled all the parts of her life in Bologna, when she added them together to make a total, would she do it all again? The answer was yes. Yes again.

But when she assembled the pieces of her immortal soul, her state of God's holy grace, her dissimulations to her father confessor, those scales that weighed her sins against her moral deeds, then the total did not have that same conviction. How forgiving was the Almighty? How merciful? Eternity was for so long.

"I was the lover," she whispered to herself.

Her reverie was broken by the commotion of her assigned husband and the labourers coming down, finishing up for the day.

"Signora, we have uncovered a problem with the strength in one of the supporting corners above the rear rooms. It was not built to support what we are now adding. We will need extra beams to go into there. Sorry, but there will be a cost."

She glanced at Borso. He nodded.

"Fine," she said, "can you give me your costing tomorrow for my approval?"

"Signora."

Borso saw them out and returned. The boss's indispensable man. She felt heavy—and smug. Her Borso would follow Cassini to the ends of the Earth.

Her Borso, who would sometimes waken her in the depth of night, to unburden his dreams, bright and fantastic tales of palaces, deserts, fierce storms, gaols, hell-fires, the prettiest of maidens and feasts of unfamiliar foods.

"You stinky and dishevelled man. I love you so much."

He smiled, that assured grin of the confident, and helped her to her feet. They stood together, around the fat belly, both heads leaning intimately over the other's shoulder and inwards to the soft neck.

Man smell.

"Don't crush your second baby," she said, in a low voice. "We need her."

"Her?" He nipped the back of Lorenna's neck with his teeth.

"Do it again," she murmured, "long and slow."

—

Cassini arrived home late one afternoon. The apartment next door had been undergoing repairs and refurbishment for a couple of months. It made the street busy and noisy, and workers were suspended on ropes from the roofline, and climbed precarious ladders and scaffolds. Some stood by, idle.

Cassini unlocked his grill bars, came inside, and made his way upstairs.

Partway up, Lorenna came running out to meet him. "Oh Gian, thank the Lord you are home."

It took a moment for her to be calm enough to tell the story.

"The Cardinal's secretary and another young priest came knocking this afternoon. I said you were not home. No one was here at all. Even the maid was at the market. Then they showed me an authority from the Cardinal to come into the house."

"You let them in?"

"I had to. They were intent on looking through everywhere."

"Right, so tell me, what were they seeking?"

"I imagined they wanted your papers and reports, and we went first to your study under the telescope dome. But they didn't spend much effort there at all. They then went through the whole house."

"Did they disturb much?"

"Very little is misplaced or disturbed. I managed to follow behind, listening as best I could."

"If they took scant interest in my papers, what were they after?"

"It seemed to me they were interested in where each person was sleeping. They inspected the little items in each person's room. I'm sorry, I couldn't stop them. It felt as though they went into every room to disguise what they were looking for."

"You're sure?"

"No. Oh, and the young monk was sent up the kitchen staircase several times."

"Lorenna, my dear, it's alright. We should have nothing to fear."

Cassini suspected they did indeed have things to fear. He would visit Battista with some urgency.

—

Gian stepped out at dawn for a brisk walk, as was his habit.

Approaching home, he was passing a man walking by.

The man paused. "Cassini? Gianni Cassini?" He waited for a response.

"Yes, I'm Cassini. Gian Cassini. And you?"

"It's Paolo, Gian. Paolo from the Abbey at Genoa."

"Oh yes, Paolo, I remember. You have grown to a man since, but I daresay I have too." Wouldn't have recognised him, he thought.

"You have a splendid memory for faces, my friend," Gian continued. "What new stories do you bring?"

"A lot has happened since those years, Gian."

"Look," said Cassini, "we are near my home. Come in and I can make you a warm tea."

In very few steps, they were at the Cassini apartment, and Gian unbolted the grill and the tall door.

"This is an impressive painting gallery, Gian. Some fine works."

"It's my wife's work, and she is doing quite well."

"Well, I'm impressed."

They walked through to the kitchen. At this early hour, the cook Bianca was sometimes out at market. But always Bianca left a kettle and cups, and embers in the stove, for when Cassini arrived from his walk. He could then make his own tea.

"What a coincidence finding you. I live based still in Genoa. This week I am visiting because my eldest has left home to work in Bologna, and I came to check he was settled. And here I meet you walking the streets."

They drank their tea in the garden.

Paolo reminded them both of some of their class masters. For most of them, Cassini could recognise their names but not much about those long-ago classes.

"Paolo, are you still in Bologna on Friday evening. You could join us for family dinner. Say five o'clock?"

"Certainly I can. That would be an unexpected pleasure."

—

"It's plain I haven't enjoyed your spectacular rise to stardom, Gian, but I've had my own adventures. And this is an agreeable wine, I must say. I have been running an art trading business selling works from Rome and Naples across to France. I sell a lot to Marseilles, but into Paris also when needed."

Celia arrived, and had caught the last of that conversation.

"Celia, my wife. This is Paolo, who was at the Abbey college with me. It's his first time to Bologna. We shared the occasional misdemeanour at the Abbey. Into the crypts even."

Paolo hesitated. "Under the chapel?'

"At the barn."

"Yes."

Borso came up the steps with Lorenna, and Gian made the introductions.

A minute later, Borso rose, signalled to Celia, and the two slipped out to the maid's servery near the back stairs. They returned shortly to rejoin and take themselves a wine and stand with their partners.

"I was congratulating your husband on his prodigious advances with his telescope discoveries," said Paolo.

"He's been fishing for the latest unannounced news," chided Gian.

"There must be a colleague benefit that twenty years of friendship should offer," returned Paolo.

"And dear Celia, this morning I was admiring your gallery downstairs. Your work has quality."

"Very well, Signor, let me stop you," she said. She was icy.

"I know you. You were here a couple of months ago in my gallery with a confederate. You wore a heavy robe and a covering hat, I remember. Even then I felt I should recognise you. I overheard your discussions last time, and I decided then that your critiques were ignorant. Well, now I do remember you, from my Genoa days. Your name is Greggorio, not Paolo. What game are you playing in my house? I consider you not welcome."

'Paolo' had no place to manoeuvre. He made his retreat. Dinner was still to be placed.

—

"Borso, thank you. You have eerie gifts." Celia addressed the others: "Our Borso sensed a fraud within seconds. It took a few minutes of him prompting me to bring back the memories. Gian, do you still think this was your old friend Paolo? With already a grown child living away from home?"

"It's not Paolo. My Paolo had a crushed finger, from his birth. Only when this man was departing did I remember that. But I have been foolish. I never dreamt such a deception was possible."

"Who was this man?" asked Lorenna.

"A plant. We'll assume an interested party paid him."

"And trained and schooled him with the historical facts, the pieces of a coherent and believable story," added Celia.

"Tonight I would be comforted to share our meal with just our family. Come, we can sit and wait for dinner. Bianca is promising the red chickpea soup again."

—

"I was very envious of her," said Celia. "She was young and attractive, but she was a brilliant painter. When we first saw her she was twenty, and she could even by then paint in a way I doubt I ever will."

The curtains were drawn, and they lay together under a warm morning sunlight. Gian leaned his arm across Celia and whispered in her ear, "But I don't have her, I have you."

"Stop. This is not about you. I'm explaining my friendship with Elisabetta Sirani. It took me a while to relax with her, not to be threatened."

"And now?"

"And now we are the closest of girlfriends. Gian, I haven't called anyone a girlfriend since Genoa days. We are sisters in art class. I'm the older sister, but she is the better painter. It's not in the way anymore. She is so warm with me.

"You know I moved my allegiance and my attendance last year to the new Bologna Women's Art Collective. It's hers. She established it herself. Most weeks she is our instructress.

"I've shared secrets with her that even you don't know. She has told me her story too, how her family has such a tradition in art. She is only the daughter, but she is the one most gifted, and they have been supportive."

"Why is she still with her family? Has she no husband or family of her own?"

"No, not yet. She's strong. She is just uncommonly dedicated to her painting. She has the skills, she has the wild poetry, and her customers compete. She has the persuasion to sell all her work, and at premium prices. Elisabetta, Betta I call her, is my model. I aim to be there one day."

"Now you can introduce us to your sister girlfriend, your model, tonight."

"I'm nervous again. Is it too late to ask Bianca if tuna is available in town today? Her stuffed polpettoni rolls on the spit are a perfect dinner for tonight." In Bologna, a fast request for quality fish was a difficult ask.

Elisabetta Sirani joined the family weekly dinner. Celia started awkward. Elisabetta had better poise, was handling the social niceties with more finesse.

"A fine wine to start?" offered Gian.

"Oh thank you, Giovanni, Gian, but I'm one of the few who don't drink any wine."

"No such an Italian exists," said Celia.

"It's easy," said Borso, "the maid can solve that in a few moments," and he went out to the servery room that joined with the kitchen stairs.

"Betta, I've never seen you with wine, you're right, but why?" asked Celia.

"I could say I don't like it, but I don't like that it messes my mind. I cherish an alertness and a clarity. I achieve more, I stay safer, and my pieces have more shine. That's my opinion.

"But Gian, with Celi I have spent many happy hours, no wine, no, but many hours sharing our lives and our dreams. Tonight it would be a delight to hear where your life has been. I know the obvious. You are the city astronomer. We all know you. But then surely we don't know you. Both of you are not from Bologna, and we know no town tales of your families.

"And Borso. And Lorenna. You are from elsewhere too. I want to learn about you all."

Maybe not all.

"We'll make it a stories night for all. A wonderful plan."

They moved to the dining table, as food had been arranged and was waiting. Stuffed tuna rolls from the kitchen spit. Seasoned with a dozen aromatic herbs and garlic and cheese, and covered with a sauce. Bianca stood to one side, wearing a discreet smile of pride.

Gian Cassini started long ago, long ago when his memories of his birth parents were faint. The disorientation and fears of a very young boy struggling to trust a new family. The sliced neck and the narrow escape from a big gang of swarthy corsair pirates along the coast under Genoa. The seductions and dubious ethics of the astrology of his youth. ("But I believe in astrology," Elisabetta said.)

Courting the Signora here, with some saucy embellishments invented.

The sombre and frightening interview with the famous Galilei on his deathbed.

Searching the islands off Venice for a glassblower who could grind a lens from its outside.

Riding for a month each way across the Alps ("And me too.") just to talk about a tiny new moon.

The ignominies of being the poor husband of a rising Bologna painter. ("I'll speak to you later!")

Even Lorenna and Borso appreciated the skill of the storymaking. Lorenna proposed a toast to the teller.

The maid cleared away the first course of food and its plates, and brought in more. A choice of two pastas, a wholemeal pasta in anchovy sauce, and a bean soup with pasta. Borso offered more wine and lemonade.

"The guest must be next," said Lorenna towards Elisabetta.

"Well, competing with Gian's story will be difficult. I'm a Bologna girl, and all my life has been about painting.

"My family have all been painters. Many of the Bolognese families are all artists. I was the eldest of four children of Margherita and Giovanni. My father had his own studio. He had been trained here by the famous Guido Reni. My father is also a merchant of art, his own a little, but more and more of other artists' works.

"And then my father trained me, in his studio. Celi, it's wrong to be falsely bashful, so let me say my art was soon judged to be good and in high demand.

"But my family are generous about that. They all encourage me and rejoice in the family reputation."

Elisabetta paused and looked to the floor.

"My customers like that my paintings are original and unafraid. And I can work fast."

"Isn't it one of the mysteries in life," said Celia, sitting next to her guest, "that some people are assigned few opportunities to succeed, and some God blesses easily? You were indeed favoured, my dearest friend."

"Can you tell us about what inspires your work?" asked Gian.

"Hmm, well let me talk about a recent canvas."

She paused.

"I called it the *Rape of Europa*."

"Not subtle."

"No, it's strong material. Not gospel. Not saint. Not even Old Testament. It's Greek gods mythology. Those pagan subjects are in high demand, despite we claim a different God. Zeus the boss god abducted Europa. Seducing humans was a common activity for him. Europa was King Minos' mother from Crete. Zeus had disguised himself as a bull, because this was another trick of his. Now why a woman should be seduced by a bull is a puzzle. Hey, my clients love these old stories."

She stopped again.

Her lips trembled and a tear rolled from one eye.

"Celi," she said, leaning over, "I can't do this."

Celia sat up in shock and put an arm around her friend.

"I can't do this anymore. It's not the truth. It's nonsense. Everything is a lie."

"What's a lie? Zeus as a bull?"

She shook her head, eyes closed.

"No, my life is a lie." Her voice was cracking.

"I'm the painter, but the story is not my story. Oh, my dear Celia, I'm so deeply sorry. I need to wait. I need to think."

She stood and walked, half ran, to the lounging room.

Celia caught Gian's eye, and both followed Elisabetta out.

Borso and Lorenna stayed to help the terrified maid salvage the meal. The fritters with elderberry flowers would have to keep until tomorrow morning.

"Celi, you are the dearest friend I have ever had. But I haven't told you my story honestly. You know only the same version as all the world knows."

They waited. She sobbed.

"I'm a girl, Celi. Girls don't get educated. You have no idea how I stormed and fought with my father before he would let me into his studio. In my dismay, I would play with shades of colour in the mud and dust. When I was ten, a friend of the family took my father to task and they staged a very angry argument. Father would train his sons, but never the girl.

"Oh, Celi, I've never told anyone this."

She paused.

"He did then train me. He was very reluctant.

"I learned. I had a gift for the art. I was very capable. My younger brothers made a game of putting a knife through some of my canvases. For a long time, my father wouldn't put anything of mine out to market. When he did, they sold easily.

"When I started attending the Bologna art group, that was the first time I felt understood."

"Betta dear, why are you not away from your family, why not married? You could escape."

"My father will not allow it, although I know many men have asked for me. Celia, did your parents choose you two?"

"No, we fell in love. Our parents surrendered. They were not unhappy, though."

"You are the exception. My father refused to consider marrying me off. He realised my art earnings were now worth too much to his family, provided I stayed at home. My father is not well now for years. He works little, and nor do my brothers. The family workshop and the merchant activities, I do most of it all. And I paint. That is the family income."

"I thought you were brave and modern, choosing your art above the distractions of a family."

"I left you to believe that. But I am bitterly lonely inside. My heart breaks. My art explores the far reaches of human experience, and the gods' too, and I live none of that for myself.

"Celi, you are my only true friend. I will lie to you no more."

—

Malvasia at Panzano retired his twenty-year-old Campani telescope from Rome and bought a newer model. It took the off-campus professor Cassini by surprise, but it was welcomed. The clarity difference was huge, and Cassini resumed more research there.

"Go back to Jupiter," advised Borso. "It's been neglected by everyone since Galilei took fright."

"Go back to Zeus," repeated Celia, in mockery. "Greek or Roman, father of all gods, go for the best."

"Start afresh," said the Marquis. "We can see as we never could before." But Malvasia didn't himself appear fresh. He was suffering pains, and his breath was short.

Cassini pointed the new weapon to Jupiter. The planet was clearer. One massive red spot and other fuzzy coloured markings were visible. It took little time to observe that Jupiter rotated every ten hours.

"Come closer," suggested Borso. "Mars."

"Prepare for war," said Celia.

Mars had real features that could be recognised at next viewing, and its rotation of 24.5 hours was also easy to find.

The observations that the planets rotated had not been difficult to make. He could document those. Other observers

                    Cassini's Vision

would follow him one day, and they would verify the same facts.

Cassini's reputation was of an accurate and pedantic recorder of precise data. Data that others could accept as highly reliable.

If the other planets were being found to be rotating, then if the Earth too were ever assumed to be a planet, was it also rotating?

A decade ago he had found his awful answer to this using the gnomon peep-hole at the Bologna basilica. It was not acceptable truth then; it was still not permissible now. The Earth had to be the centre of our universe. It was not a planet of the Sun. That was from Holy Writ. That was the Roman judgement.

He had never published the gnomon conclusion.

He would publish his observations this time on the planet rotations, but he would not comment one word more on any added conclusions.

But Giovanni Cassini had one further problem.

His measurements kept showing a discrepancy in planet timings, disparities in the precise moments that the Jupiter moons went into eclipse, crossed before or behind the planet. The eclipse events ought to be exactly measurable, and very predictable. He knew his Euclid, he knew how to calculate across vast space.

Those timings in his recorded events varied through the year, like a clock that couldn't keep proper time. Across several months the eclipses lagged further behind what might otherwise be expected. Then they began to pick up again. This was strange.

"It's as though the light from the planets is delayed when Jupiter is on the far side past the Sun. It suggests the light has a finite speed crossing the heavens," he complained to Borso. "Up to twenty minutes delayed."

"Conceivably light does have a speed. Perhaps it is not instant."

"That's not possible," said Cassini.

"It might be possible," whispered Celia in bed. The scientific detail was too much for her, but watching the processing and the agony in Gian's soul and mind, that she did relate to. "It may be that that's the truth. New and never known before."

"It's not possible," he said.

It wasn't possible.

The Earth would be circling the Sun!

It was just not plausible.

She held him. Urgently.

It was not possible. Light was an instant thing. Light doesn't need time to travel across vast distances. Any concept of a measurable "speed of light" was only a nonsense. Another explanation was needed for his anomalies.

Again he would document his reports, the reports that gave him reputation, fame and modest family wealth. He would attest to his observed data, and leave it for someone later to digest its meanings.

—

Cassini found another comet. The last one he saw was eleven years ago, and that one had faded from view after little more than a month. He'd published all he had observed that time, and would do so again now.

But he was on his own this time. They had buried the Marquis Cornelio Malvasia a few weeks ago.

He immediately sent advice on his comet finding to London, to the new *Royal Society*.

He had judged England's future wrong. England had steadied. It had a king again, and King Charles II had approved a royal charter for the world's first academy of science and philosophy. This was the institutional academy that Huygens and Wren and many of the invisible Republique had dreamed of.

But, thought Cassini, London was far, far from Italy.

Meanwhile, he now had his second comet to investigate. Was it safe now to be comparing, to be guessing some common features? It was now the age of telescopes and stable clocks, and of a mathematics that could triangulate on planets and their cousins. Soon it might be possible to predict and explain these renegade objects, or just to describe their trajectories, even if more understanding was lagging.

Their path, the little that could be seen, was part of a circle, or similar, but not centred on Earth or Sun. The centre of their circle was far into space, beyond the planets. Was that feasible? Every theory from Aristotle and Ptolemy to Copernicus and Galilei, rest his soul, had heavenly bodies circling the Earth or the Sun. Huygens' Luna Saturni, his "titan", still went around its massive master. What big body was centre of a comet's circle?

Johannes Kepler had years ago suggested the planets traced elliptical orbits around the Sun, stretched circles. He could not explain why that should be, and, tainted with the hysteria over Copernicus' theories he built on, Kepler was put aside.

Cassini built his own proposal. The two comets could both be on a circular orbit, centred on an unknown and likely never discoverable point beyond where the planets circled. And that mysterious centre was from Earth off in the direction of the star Sirius.

He had no proofs. He had no explanation.

He had a sampling of only two comets to consider.

Cassini went to publication. In all Europe, no one yet had anything better to offer.

"What is truth?" asked Celia.

That night Lorenna held him. Gently. Long and languorous. From Venezia with love.

No, he would not move to London.

What is truth? Giovanni Cassini did not know.

—

Cassini sent Borso to The Hague. Christiaan Huygens was using a new configuration of telescope lenses that gave better images than ever before.

Borso would take personal delivery of a set of these lenses. He was keen to build them himself into a new telescope.

He would not be returning for about two months.

Lorenna fretted.

Cassini worked with no assistant for the side tasks.

Celia spent more time at the Women's Collective.

"We've had no Elisabetta the past two weeks," she complained to Gian. "She was ill some weeks ago with a violent stomach pain, and we thought she had got over that.

"She came in for a few minutes today, but wouldn't stay. Gian, she looked awful. She has lost a lot of weight, and she has no confidence at all, not the Betta we know."

A month later, Elisabetta Sirani died in Bologna, in much pain and illness. Her fingers had become purple. She was a skeleton with little flesh.

The family doctor diagnosed death by poison. However, a dozen stories and rumours spread through the town assigning blame on the housemaid, on jealous men, on pregnancy gone wrong. Celia believed the doctor.

What all agreed was that the early death of one of their best ever artists was a tragedy. Her body was displayed in tribute at the basilica, and the Cassinis attended the massive public funeral where Bologna gathered to grieve, and to honour her.

Celia the girlfriend was heartbroken.

# Bologna

Borso was overdue. Lorenna became more concerned. It was the eleventh week after Borso left.

A message arrived to Bologna saying a ship was being held at quarantine alongside Genoa. Cassini made haste to Genoa with one horse.

A galleon was indeed offshore, flying the yellow jack, the flag of disease.

Cassini found stabling, and walked to the harbourmaster, whence he was referred to a small office holding passenger lists. It took time to jostle to the front of the fretting and noisy crowd.

Borso Gordeo? Yes, Signor, a Gordeo is aboard.

Signor, we have a single case of plague onboard. She hasn't died, but she is quarantined in cabin, and we are pleased she is recovering. We believe all else are not infected.

London, Signor. They have a problem starting there.

The official had called this information countless times.

Signor, we plan to release everyone else in two days, provided the peste is not spreading. We are not proposing a full quaranta, the full forty days.

Thank you, Signor, that is very generous of you.

In two days, Cassini had arranged two horses and a horseman, and in mid-afternoon, the ship's passengers were disembarked.

"Gian, get me off that water. I want to go home."

They made favourable progress and found an inn at nightfall.

Next day, and back at Bologna, Borso unpacked his treasures.

"You still sure you can build me a telescope from these?"

"Of course. It will be a long one though. Huygens still makes his lenses for long instruments. But tonight I am tired. I must sleep first."

Borso slept late.

Lorenna checked him. He still slept.

Lorenna checked him once more.

"Gian, Gian, I am worried. I think he has an ache to the head, and a fever."

Each looked into his room, and left.

They were fearful.

An hour later they checked again. They closed the door.

Plague.

Celia threw her arms about and screeched in pain. "Franchooo!" she screamed. She returned to the closed door and pummelled it. Gian and Lorenna looked at each other in dismay and confusion, and they took Celia to sit down, still hysterical. Children ran in, followed by the nanny in pursuit.

"Lisbeth, take the kids, please, now!" and the mother hen fetched her chickens away.

Celia quietened. She said to Lorenna, "Draw me lots, Renna, for who attends him."

"He should go to the Lazaretto hospital out East of the city, the Jerusalem side," said Gian. "He mustn't stay here."

"He does stay here. He is the only case in Bologna. We can control this." Lorenna drew her shoulders back. "And Celia, I will not draw lots with you. For this time he is my husband. I will be with my husband, and if needed I will perish with him."

     Cassini's Vision

They instituted a regime where only Lorenna entered Borso's room. She sat with him and mopped his fever. Cloths and water and later some food for her were exchanged carefully at the door. They placed herbs and oils of the strongest scents inside the door to overcome the miasmas, the bad airs: rosemary, mint, garlic, chopped onions.

Lorenna left the room only twice in her vigil.

She couldn't give much assistance. His skin blotched in heavy dark welts. His manhood swelled as though an egg grew there, and his armpits too, and these were cause of much pain. He spoke for a while as in a trance, muttering, "They are there. We must look, we must look, they are there so cold in the black mud," and she dismissed it as the fading phantom of her man.

Otherwise, he moved little, and he neither ate nor drank. He vomited a trace of blood. She chose to leave it uncleaned for now, because the solution was a large job, and it would not help him. His body became mottled black all over.

Lorenna did not sleep, but she knew she would not have him back. She fingered her rosary beads for all her internment.

In thirty hours her Borso was dead.

Three hours later, she left the room, undressed, putting her things aside for disposal, and washed her body at length. In her own bed, she curled to her side, naked, and sobbed in bottomless sorrow. Then she slept for a very long time.

Celia had kept out of Borso's room as agreed, but she had busied herself with cleaning, many times, all the rest of the house. She had never been an assiduous cleaner. Borso's cat followed her, as though appointed on special duty. When at last Lorenna had slept, Celia slept too.

Gian helped the maid prepare a breakfast. The maid left.

"We now have a problem. Even if only we could imagine neither Renna nor others of us have the peste, we still have a body. The Lazaretti officers as yet know nothing. Where do we proceed from here?"

"I put it that no one knows Borso has returned to Bologna," said Celia.

"True. Are you suggesting something?"

The three of them covered themselves and wrapped the body, smelling repulsively, in broad sheets.

All were concerned whether the dead man's vapours were as risky to them as living breathing vapours, but no one would share that aloud.

For hours, Gian dug a deep grave in the garden court. They carried Borso and made a clandestine family burial, all the while trying to dispose of any contamination. Clothes, bedding, the rosary beads, too, went into the grave. If they failed, there would be deaths and monumental scandal.

No priest. No service. But the complete body of Borso was still safe for its resurrection in the final days of Earth.

In the coming months, Borso was reported as never having returned from a trip he had taken to far Europe. His fate was not known. The household grieved and could not reveal.

—

Gian's two eldest lived by now in Genoa, having gone home to their roots. The younger children had not seen the burial. Any reference to plague had been avoided. Borso had died suddenly, and was gone.

Two weeks after the death, the total family, Cassini and Gordeo, gathered for a private and secret grieving ritual. They brought their reminders.

A low table with one candle sat in the centre of the room.

Lorenna placed on the table a terracotta cat. "He had bought it in Crete," she said. "It was his first awkward courting gift to me, because he knew I had been in Crete as a child. I talked with him about cats, and he told me the sailors always believed that those ships with cats aboard were less likely to come to any misfortune."

As if on cue, Borso's cat strolled into the room.

"It was I who encouraged him to bring Cat into our house."

Cat moved into the centre and sat.

"I think our cat should have a real name," said Gian. He looked at Lorenna.

"Could it be proper that a lesser creature should have a name?" She thought a while. "But I will name him Borsino."

Every child brought a toy, and every one of those intricate and beautiful toys had been fabricated, carved, fashioned by Borso in his idle moments.

The Genoa two, Lucia and Piero, brought their memories of the other man in the house and in Dad's Observatory, the one who would talk with them at times Dad would not.

Giovanni placed on the table Borso's quadrant astrolabe and the old ship's compass.

"This was Borso's successful ploy on the day he applied to me for employment. This point ... here ... was his success. He became family."

He glanced at Celia.

"But also, Borso was my solid colleague, and he could make me anything I asked."

"Except a new telescope."

"Except one last instrument. We all one day will have one last task we never get to."

Celia faltered. She looked to Lorenna, but Lorenna was sobbing.

She put on the table a Persian hookah.

Celia was now sobbing too.

"And yes, we did. Long back when we were silly."

She placed out a rolled parchment written in foreign cursive script.

"And no, this we never did. Not yet."

Celia held in her hand another item, a child's small locket. It had been a gift from Anna. Celia decided that this story was hers only, and she made no mention.

Celia walked a long time after the ceremony was finished. Her heart grew hard and dry and angry. "God of the Heaven," she cried in her soul, "you still lie to me. Where is your truth?"

—

Borso's cleaned-out room was left bare.

Widow Lorenna dismissed the nanny, and took to keeping all the children, her two and Celia's later daughter Carla, along the mezzanine with her. She set about schooling them all herself. It gave a structure and a discipline to her daily life.

Still, she was part of the household, ate with them, organised the house affairs. But a sadness was beneath the surface always. Her soul had moved aside, thought Gian. She would be with them and her eyes would move to far away, then return, and she would resume the conversations.

From Gian she sought no close comfort. Her current state was still an inner dialogue with her husband. Gian waited, stayed patient, hoping time would soften the pain. However, Lorenna never asked him down.

Celia carried her grief differently. Her intemperate but private passions with Borso had had most of their heat ten and twenty years ago, and the household had given them blessing.

But Lorenna had been correct, Lorenna was Borso's wife. His widow. Celia still loved him, but in death he was Lorenna's.

Lorenna did at times talk quietly with Celia when the two were alone. Sad sisterly conversations, musings, memories, tears. Comparisons.

The dynamic of the connections between them all was different now. It could never return to what they had once known.

But life went on. The extended family was not broken beyond retrieval. It was scarred. Its task was to heal.

Celia painted with a frenzy, apocalyptic and dark, and she was again writing some unreadable poetry.

Gian taught, observed, wrote, researched. Alone. He had no thoughts at this time of any replacement "butler".

Lorenna raised kids and did the books. And sat by herself, or with Borsino the cat, more often. She would stand at a window, and stare down, down to the garden below.

Celia wanted Gian's bed most nights, to hold him.

One evening after dinner, Lorenna asked, "Gian, I have a request."

"Sure."

"I've never been to the Teatro Anatomico. I've heard you mention you have been there long ago. I'd like to go one day.

"No, don't take panic. I'd been thinking on how my poor Borso's body so fast changed from a healthy man to a corpse. So quickly, before my terrified eyes."

"We are so, so sorry, my dear Renna," said Celia.

"I'm coping—I think. It was all too abrupt!"

"The Teatro di Anatomia?" He had indeed visited the Theatre many times, mostly to be measuring and assessing to help build himself a high standard astronomy lecture hall in Panzano Villa. Not ever so grandiose, not as large, but still stealing style and functionality. Before Lorenna's arrival to Bologna.

"Would you take me there, Gian? Or would you both take me there?"

"Of course we can, if that's what you want."

"I could get us into a class," said Gian, "but if we wait for January, in about six weeks, it will be Carnival, and the public has easier access."

"Six weeks away is fine. Thank you. I want to look inside who we deeply are. This might help."

It was a month later, when the evening was late, that the three of them were sitting in silence by candlelight arranging pieces of a large puzzle on the tabletop.

Celia put her hand on Gian's arm for a moment.

"Gian," said Celia, "Renna wants you tonight."

He was instantly confused. He had grown used to Lorenna no longer needing him. Life moves along, inevitably changing over time.

But Lorenna was sitting opposite him. Now. At the same table.

"Lorenna would like your company tonight. I want you to be very gentle with her."

Lorenna looked sheepishly at Cassini, and a small wry smile was on her face. She shrugged her shoulders, and that shy smile remained. The woman from Venice. Tears welled in his eyes, and his belly dissolved. She held her hand out across the table, and Gian reached and took it.

"Well!" he said.

"Yes, well," she replied.

"Go," said Celia. "I love you both."

—

Every family has quirks and habits that defy expected logic.

Cassini was in Bianca's kitchen sharpening the knives, three of them. He still used a stone he had found as a youth in a creek near Genoa. Bianca had long ago accepted that Gian sharpened her knives. She told her market gossip group, and they had been concerned for her.

Uncle Antonio as a hobby had from time to time hunted and trapped small game out of town: hare, fox, sometimes boar. The knife was one of the tools of that trade. Gian went with him several times, but he had not adopted hunting as his own passion. Only the knife sharpening stayed with him.

Bemused? Yes. But Bianca was flattered at the service. Gian talked personally to each blade, caressing it, testing it, sharpening more.

Only Celia was nervous about his knife fetish. He didn't know why. It wasn't a jealousy or suspicion thing. She carried her own dagger at times.

"I do like my knives sharp," the cook said. "Meat cuts more easily."

"I have no problem with your meals, Bianca. Not at all."

"Well, this week I am getting special practice cutting off the fatty parts, too. Our market butcher is teaching us to collect the animal fat and boil it. Next week we learn to make ash water, so now I'm saving the fireplace ash, too."

"The butcher, the meat seller, wants you to not throw away the ash from the stove? Bianca, that's tallow and lye. I know that. That's soap."

She grinned. "I am learning to make our own soap. It can replace that cleaning soda the maid leaves in your room."

Today it was the welcoming and crusty smell of Bianca's loaves that were all through the kitchen, and wafting afield.

"Do you ever write a diary, Bianca?"

He knew his mistake the moment he had spoken: Bianca did not read. Then how did she cope with market buying?

He would fudge his way out, not wait for the awkwardness to even get a start.

"I've decided to write everything I've ever done into one big book. I have a new project. You will need to keep me fed for weeks."

"Signor Cassini, you are famous. My market friends are envious I work for you. I think a few weeks will not be enough time to write all your discoveries."

"Hah, most was written long ago. I will collect it together." He did have a lot of diary notes. He would pass most to a scribe for copying. Check it through. Send it to that new printing press in Bologna. It should be finished in short order.

Why does she not ask, What for?

Servants have barriers, and such things are not said, he decided.

Bianca placed a cup of tea and an end crust of hot bread in front of her master.

"Bianca, we never know, do we, if one sad day we might die unexpectedly. It would be a shame to have wasted a life's work. Someone might have used my discoveries, but I had forgotten to write them."

"Signor, you can't talk like that."

No, he thought.

A month later, Cassini published his collected life memoirs and earlier-published work, his *Opera Astronomica*.

Few noticed.

—

Gian arranged for three entrance passes for two days at the public dissection, the short opening day and day five. The start day was scheduled for the Tuesday, but that could depend on a corpse being available.

Battista Riccioli dropped in on Sunday. Sunday was the Lord's day of rest, but the church Father seldom forced himself to stay home if he could think of business or interest anywhere. He stepped in from the cold with a theatric bow and a sweep of his hat.

"Came to wish you all an enjoyable dissection. I had thought you were about to have a late start this week," he said. "We have no qualifying homeless people dying just now."

"But now? They will start on time?" Celia had never been to a Teatro performance either.

                    Cassini's Vision

"Yes, Signora, they will. I believe the governor has over-ruled a prisoner's life sentence, and ordered he be hanged in gaol tomorrow. Fine-bodied lad, pleasant spectacle. This is not public knowledge, but it does avoid complications."

She looked bemused.

"And then I'll be on my way. You are prepared for a major performance, I presume? This is not clinical on Tuesday, it's theatric."

"I'm told."

The Archiginnasio in Bologna was the central and congregate building constructed a hundred years ago in the time of the Council of Trent. The time of total overhaul of Catholicism and the Law. The time of defence to the ravages of Protestantism. The time of consolidating and controlling the schools of the Law and the Arts and Sciences. The time when the University became whole, encompassed, unified.

Bologna's University had since then outgrown that one enormous gymnasium complex, but the rebuilt Anatomy Theatre was inside, in prime place. It was built there in the last thirty years "in the interests of the splendour, the decoration and the honorific needs of the public, the schools and the whole city," ignoring cost.

Because the world's birthplace of the Anatomy Theatre was Bologna.

Padua's Anatomy Theatre, Rome Anatomy Theatre, all the other Italian such theatres were smaller, more functional, more austere. The rest of Europe had started copying those prim, standing-room, even temporary Anatomy Theatres, but the one in Bologna stayed grand, proud and unique.

Lorenna and her two escorts walked through the immense doorway. The Theatre was a blaze of candle-lit colour. The walls were all panelled in fine strongly scented cedar, with statues of past doctors and dignitaries of the recent and the far past. Gods and zodiac carvings and paintings covered all the ceiling. All the tiered seating for several hundred people was cushioned and draped with coloured hang-overs.

Below and in front of the tiers were a marble table, empty, and a high lecturing podium, also vacant.

The attendant checked their tickets, and escorted them to the second-from-front row, an excellent viewing position.

They were early. The front row began filling with robed academics whose field related to anatomy or medical. Cassini was an academic, and he wore his robes, but astronomy had less claim to rank here today.

Others in his second row were from other cross disciplines. This event was entertainment: the real medical students had their separate non-public expert classes, more pertinent for them, during study seasons.

Battista strolled in from the other doorway, and sat himself directly in front of Cassini.

He turned around to speak to the three.

"Ah, yes, I forgot to tell you." His eyes carried mischief.

The row behind filled with students. And then the noise level rose abruptly, as the public was allowed to storm into the top seats. Some seemed to have wandered in from the other Carnival activities of the day. A few wore their masks.

Lastly four officials, in the finest of all the robes, entered and sat on the reserved seats alongside and under the podium, facing the crowd, and on the far side of the slab.

The audience settled.

The master of the house entered carrying the official rod, stood, and thumped on the floor. All fell silent, including the rabble behind. The lector entered, climbed to his podium, and sat. His robes today were simple, but no one here took that as lack of prestige. The professor lector runs this event.

Still no cadaver was on the bench.

One person uttered a comment from the rear. The lector pointed to him without a word, and a guard promptly removed the offender. The silence was now total.

   Cassini's Vision

After the obligatory welcomes and the dignitary and colleague recognitions, the professor asked more silence while the corpse was brought in.

Eight strong youths in uniform trundled in a trolley with a second marble slab and a draped corpse. They lifted the heavy new slab and placed it exactly on top of the fixed one. The lads retired, and two autopsy surgeons came and stood at each end of the body, ready, awaiting the professor's instructions.

A trumpet shattered the silence, from high in the rear corner, with an ode to signal the event open.

With a hand wave, the professor signalled his attendants to remove the shroud. There lay a fine body of a man, possibly in his 20s, clean and shaven.

"Can't see neck bruises," whispered Celia.

But the skin from his neck to his testicles, and the skin along his four limbs, had been cut longwise, and the ends of those lines then cut crossways. Five major skin areas had been rolled back as ten flaps of untanned leather, and his belly and limbs were opened for all to see.

The crowd inhaled as one.

For three hours, the professor both demonstrated his corpse, and played with the audience. He never left his podium.

He called and the surgeon pointed. He ordered, and the surgeons sliced off two belly skins and threw them like flat-bread dough. He asked, and a surgeon eased out an organ. He tutored the audience to call the correct names for all the visible parts as the surgeon pointed to one bone or organ after another.

This was chapter one of the book of the body.

He allowed a few minute stop, a quick relief break, and then the lector continued the event.

They had seen the obvious organs, they had tried out their names. Now he spent an hour sketching what those parts did, how they connected.

Lastly, he elicited disease names from his audience, and made a basic story for each, connecting it with one of those organs, again demonstrating with the corpse on his table.

Other than slicing some skin, they had cut nothing more. That would start tomorrow. There would be ten days total, some with twenty hours of dissection. They would explore more of this body, discussing and arguing aspects both fleshly and philosophical.

"On Saturday, we will have a female body."

A few gasps erupted.

The trumpet blew, and the lector descended, bowed and departed.

Battista turned around to Giovanni, grinning. "Good free entertainment! Day one is so low-brow! The professor and his two puppets."

"That was amazing," said Celia. "Clearly much more is there to learn, though. We should have booked more days."

They looked to Lorenna. "Just take me home," she said.

"No, not yet," said the Battista. "I want to buy us all a hot drink. I have a favourite inn down in the square."

They stepped down the stairs into the cool, and the priest led them to his chosen coffee house in the Piazza Maggiore. It was not yet the end of the daylight. The Carnival mob were noisy in the streets still.

"Isn't coffee still the bitter spirit of Lucifer?" asked Lorenna.

"No, I don't think so. Even the Pope has approved coffee now," countered Battista. "Ah, we all must take note of that approval. But I just like the coffee."

"Gian, taste the coffees for me, and hand me your pick," Lorenna conceded.

"Father, who was the cassocked cleric up front who wasn't listed in the introductions?"

"Not sure, Celia. It might have been the Cardinal's deacon. Not important, I guess. He's always there."

"My stomach isn't taking well to this coffee," said Celia.

"Well, I could get accustomed to this one," said Lorenna.

"Get used to it in the mornings. Taking it late can keep you from sleeping well."

Cassini grinned. He had suffered many late nights at the telescope at Panzano, kept alert by the Count's coffee.

—

Cassini raised it again later with Riccioli.

"What did you make of your first public dissection at the Theatre?" asked Battista.

"Such a provocative event. Morbid and grand."

"Agreed."

"But we went to only the first day, as I presume you found out. Lorenna couldn't face our second one for the Saturday."

A pause.

"So, this Cardinal's deacon?"

"Father Corrando. Dominican."

"Yes, the Dominican. Evidently you know him."

"So?" Battista looked up and frowned.

"This fellow wasn't acknowledged in the regular way."

Battista paused.

"Corrando is Inquisition. I had a watcher there for the following days too, but no one would have spotted him or her."

"Or her?"

"I keep low.

"Gian, the Inquisition watches everything, judges everything. If any of the proceedings should become spiritually deviant, if anything heretical arose, Corrando would have intervened in the ceremony. He would have stood to demand the professor publicly defend his position."

"That wasn't explained."

"Are you surprised?"

"Superintendent of State Waters," he reported.

Gian had returned late last night from the Cardinal's mansion at Florence. Lorenna, her morning tea and porridge not yet finished, was relieved. She had feared Gian may not return from the meeting. Giovanni had developed a mortal fear of all things Florence.

"In the end," he said, "it was an easy trip, easy ride."

"Another job? What state waters?"

"Superintendent of State Waters for all Papal States."

"I think this Pope wants your allegiance."

"Yes, you are right. An offer was also made that I should take Holy Orders, become a priest."

"Gian! How?"

"Leave Bologna, and divorce Celia."

"They can't do that."

"Oh, it gets called an annulment, decreed never proper from the first."

"You and Celi, you've always been proper. Oh, Gian. They are playing with you."

"I said no. Will not happen."

She sat. He sat beside her and put his arm around her shoulder as she wept.

"Celi is unwell again this week," she sniffed. "She vomits often now. The hardness in the side of her belly was never any baby, and it is hurting her so."

"I'll go to her now."

"She's asleep on her bed in her studiola. I've placed aromatic oils there for her. Look in," she said, "but leave her undisturbed. Old Borsino is keeping her company."

—

She seldom went to her Artist Academy, just stayed home. She was cheerful. Her studio room was reminding

Gian of a smaller front room studio they long ago loved in a harbourside home in Genoa.

The hardness sickness commonly made its victim thin and drawn, and then frail. Celia had always owned a slim body. She got no thinner in the following months. The vomits abated.

Life resumed to some normality in the Cassini household.

Until New Year's Day.

She left behind three short notes. The studiola was neatly arranged. Each note was attached to an artwork beautifully mounted, each hanging on its own wall. Her last gifts of love.


*Gian, my champion, my soul's partner in truth, my hero. Stay looking.*

*I loved you dearly. Thank you.*

Gian's art gift he recognised. It was the tiny triptych. Her hidden soul.

The next ...


*Lorenna, my sister in love, my sharer in fortune. Stay loving.*

*I loved you dearly. Thank you.*

And ...


*Borso, my passion, my spirit, my light. I am coming, my dreamer.*

*I loved you dearly. Thank you.*

One other planned token remained. A private one. Giovanni found in his room a model Genoese galleon, old, not one he had seen. The model had no keel; it was flat to sit on a table.

Celia had never sailed. Nothing braver than a Venice gondola.

Gian, what's actually out there? Past the outrageous Venice? Across the wild seas? What unknown empires? What's above this Earth? Beyond your last planet Saturn? What's the real truth, Gian? Cassini sat in his room for hours holding the little galleon. Under its flat bottom was one small letter "f", but Cassini could fathom no meaning in that.

She had left in his trust her last secrets.

They never saw again that woman with the reputation, the savvy and the fire. Her search. A little magic and some courage.

How she went, where she went, they never knew.

Gian began his year of tears.

—

Cassini had lost his loyal attendant to a presumed misadventure on the seas. He had lost his wife to sickness. His family was just Lorenna.

Son Andro, now twenty, had after the loss of his mother moved to Rome to begin studies for taking Holy Orders.

Three children remained at home, age on the cusp of double figures, Lorenna's two—she had lost the third—and Celia's Carla. They were now all in appropriate care of the resident nanny.

Lorenna stayed most of her days alone in her room or in the courtyard. She prayed for her soul. She slept by herself. Mornings, she would eat a breakfast, but didn't appear for other meals, and Bianca brought food to her room.

—

Cassini spent more time with the children. They also were confused and restless, although they did watch out for each other, console each other. The house was empty, and bright days were harder to conjure up.

One morning he had news for Lorenna. Would it be welcome news?

"The siege of your Crete is over. The naval raids have stopped."

Lorenna nodded, said nothing.

"A treaty was signed a few days ago. Venice surrendered. Sorry."

"Gian, it's twenty-five years since I left there. It's not my Crete now."

"No, it's Ottoman Crete." The richest foreign possession of Venice, but no more.

"Gian, my love, listen to me." She was fighting back tears. "We need to talk."

Alarmed, he sat at the table.

"Gian, my soul is so anxious. You can see that. I'm not happy."

"Of course I know. You're lost where I cannot reach."

Lorenna began sobbing. Deep, bottomless sobbing.

Bianca walked in from the servery, stopped, and crept back out.

Giovanni was also weeping quietly.

They were one each side of the family gathering table.

# Paris

Gian arranged the formal adoption of Lorenna's two. With Celia's Carla, he now had three children at home. At least from the wreck could emerge a smaller family with a tighter family future.

The broken and suffering Lorenna had departed, and she had entered the local convent. Gian had all the children.

The Bologna Senate called him to an interview.

He deferred for a week, sweating and agonising, consulting and consoling with only himself. Was his commission to be terminated? Unlikely, as they had been respectful of his research and reports, and the name of Bologna had been surely enhanced.

Was it an Inquisition trap? Had Battista's backroom defences weakened?

His household, that flourishing family and its attendants and its social amiability, had wound up, but sometimes vigilantes can pull tasty scandal from things now historic.

Then he reported to interview as he knew he must.

The Senate president welcomed him, congratulated him on the quantity and prestige of the many superb projects he had brought to Bologna.

The next word would be "But".

"But we have a problem."

"Signor President?"

"Paris wants to steal you from us."

"Signor?"

"We have a direct request from King Louis, no less, asking a loan of your services for two years. He has ordered the construction of a Paris Observatory. He wants you in Paris as his exclusive overseer of all design and construction. What's unfortunate for us is that Pope Clement has signalled his approval already, provided we lose you for those years only. You are then to return here. King Louis has played his game with cunning."

Cassini stood and walked aside. "Sorry, Signor, a moment to cope."

If ever was a time when a move might be an appropriate choice, it was now.

"A generous salary for you, accommodation, and a suitable travel allowance. They do want you."

—

Cassini returned to Bologna two years later. The Observatory was finished. He had fought with the architects, struggled with his French, and triumphed. No expert architect, French or other, will ever build a satisfactory Observatory without knowing astronomy.

He had also spent much of his Paris time with Louis' fledgling *Académie des Sciences*, meeting in the king's court library. Now he was a Fellow of that academy. The Sun King had loved inviting Cassini to his court; he wanted to hear exciting stories of astronomical observations, and often he invited along also the queen and his princes and dukes. Stay with the facts, Gian had learned, but work the facts into a dramatic story. And learn precisely that fastidious court etiquette that Louis insisted on.

To King Louis' last proposition, Cassini had not yet made formal reply. He had begged two months' grace. But his heart knew he would not be leaving his Italy again, risks though it still held.

While he had been away, he had arranged the Bologna house was painted and refurbished.

He employed new house staff. Bianca was not available —he had put aside a suitable pension for her two years ago, but she had returned to her brother's household, and she was now quite unwell.

He set about contacting old friends, re-establishing the Italian lives of his three children. Soon he must prepare lecture schedules, find staff, assess the telescope and instrument maintenance, and so resume University duties, even the Papal engineering. He had to rebuild a life.

Two messengers arrived to Cassini, an hour apart. The first delivered him a sealed letter. The second came to inform him Father Giovanni Battista Riccioli had just died. Riccioli had suffered a short illness and died in peace.

The sealed heavy letter from the first messenger was fully waxed and stamped. Inside was another, again waxed, sealed and dated.

The first said, *"Farewell my friend. It's your turn. Your war must now be your own. Read and burn. Regards GBR."*

The inner one read, *"Giovanni, these are pages torn from my private journals of past years. No one has ever read them. The other pages I burned today, but these I will share with you. Be shocked if you must, but they contain my soul. This soul I fear may be not what you saw. Your Celia was right. Always search further. We never understand it all, but we can always learn more. Always something is beyond where we see.  B."*


<u>*Dated 1658.*</u>

*My God, my God, why hast thou forsaken me?*

*My heart is empty. My soul is dry. My body is lonely.*

*I must write so that my thoughts can make a sense.*

                                          Cassini's Vision

*I visited the Cassinis again yesterday. My shame and confusion are now great. All at home was Signora Lorenna, and she supped graciously with me, and listened to a little of my petty woes. A gout and a poor digestion that ail me sometimes. By Lucifer himself, those troubles are not what ache my soul. They are but tokens for the real.*

*And I looked on this fine woman, the woman of man Borso, and I saw someone so beautiful, so luscious and curved of body, so complete with the mother carer nature, so competent and friend of all. I desired her and sweated most unfortunately. I wished to take her, and her me, while the house was empty, and to know a lusty energetic happiness, both of us. That is the woman I see every time, but yesterday I was so ready to be breaking my priest vows.*

*I left in a hurry, and she didn't understand.*

*Why am I a priest of Rome? Because my father wished it so. I am well educated, and I live in a city I think the world's best. I want for no food, no luxury, no fine place to live. For my allegiance to the Rome regime, I am paid well. I have even a collection of science instruments that the young boy still within me can delight in—I need only to make good reports that can shine prestige on my Order.*

*My Order! A political community intent on its own success and wealth. I can believe in it no longer.*

*My spirit is dry.*

*Lorenna, my desire.*

*But Lorenna is the family of my dearest friend Giovanni C. What shame for me if my passions burst into disaster.*

*In Rome they are scheming Giovanni's disgrace, before he can bear stronger witness to the works of Copernicus. He cannot know how often I have presented his reports and findings, those parts of his findings that give him no risk, merely to blunt the forces working towards him.*

*Giovanni, I am sorry. You will never know how sorry.*


<u>*Dated 1662.*</u>

*Celia C. came to me today. I was not expecting her. She arrived passioned and she left angry. I was berated for making jests at her home on her son Andro. It was never to happen again. That woman can be a tigress.*

*I was surprised thoroughly by her tantrum and its subject. And now I must wonder, despite I was forbidden, why she fears so much that her boy has curled hair. That hair I should think would be attractive to any Italian lass in years to come. It should be an asset.*

*I should put the issue out of my head.*

*But I am lying. Lying to myself. Now I know exactly. I am a priest, therefore I never divulge. What nonsense is this? A corruption lies here, and I never can tell?*


<u>*Dated 1663.*</u>

*Giovanni C. is evil. His household is a den of immorality. He tells me lies, but I am not blind. Those children are crossbred in iniquity, in shamelessness. What transpires with devils of Hell when all guests go home?*

*But no, those devils of Hell I don't believe any longer. Then, say it this way, what exists there is a human cesspit.*

*Can I stay silent when such depravity is among us? If we all should descend to that, the races of humanity would be barbarians.*

*And to myself, what would "descend" mean? Who is to judge what is "up"? What is "up"?*

*GC I have protected you. For years I have. I think I cannot this time.*


<u>*Dated 1666.*</u>

*My friend GC is a lucky man. Yes, still my friend.*

*He had been in Florence last week. I found today there had been planned a totally unpleasant encounter with a band of "unknown brigands" along the return forest track.*

*It seems he fell in with several other friendly travellers, and the ambush was abandoned.*

*My sources are getting slower.*


<u>*Dated 1670.*</u>

*In this my journal, I have wrestled with my soul.*

*The fight has stopped. My soul, I doubt I have one. Lucifer did not win my soul; I doubt we have a Lucifer.*

*For my own mind, I will summarise herein what now I know. The world is unrecognisable from all I knew before. I believe I see now the truth. I have a peace, nay a resignation, I never knew.*


<u>*I Believe:*</u>

*I was taught the five rational proofs that God exists. They are mere casuistry.*

*The God of our theology, eternal, all-wise, all-powerful, all-merciful, is a contradiction.*

*Any God who was all-merciful and loving could not allow or ordain such widespread human misery and sin.*

*Any God who was all-powerful would not be so powerless in the face of human sin and error.*

*Any God who was infinite would not need and beg so ineffectually for human adoration and conformance.*

*The Church of priests, ours now, or any of other times and places, uses religion to control the poor and simple.*

*No God has made us. Man has fashioned the God with a fanciful collection of human traits, but taken to extreme.*

*We never were created perfect once, to then "fall" in original sin, and to need redemption to recover.*

*Our people are commanded be subservient in this conflicted life. We promise them rewards in the afterlife. But no afterlife will exist.*

*We pray to our God, who asks adoration and promises to respond to prayers. No response comes from any God ever.*

*The "mysteries" of religion are only useful for the priest class to hold power.*

*Many religions exist, believing incompatible things, and hating each other, and each insists it is the only true one.*

*All religions came from the past eras of barbarity.*

*Religions are always allied with the ruling class, and so are against the humble interests of the people.*

　　　　Cassini's Vision

*The universe is not made for the benefit of man. It just exists. As do we. We can explore and use that universe as we choose.*

*I have no spirit mysterious soul. I am just who I see I am.*

*No judge in a Heaven looks on our deeds and judges us against his arbitrary rule book.*

*It is sad, I suppose, that also no judge above watches us do good things, love each other, and avoid harming.*

*I am one of these priests I despise. It's too late for me to be not a priest. My life is mostly done, and I am not brave.*

*But I don't believe.*


*Shame. I might have had more fun.*

—

Cassini was indeed shocked. He crossed himself repeatedly. Every page he fed to the fire and burned.

Some discovered truths cannot be accepted.

For an hour he sat beside his desk, eyes closed, his elbows on his knees and his hands holding his forehead.

He stood and walked to his window and watched for a while on his Bologna streetscape below. His Bologna.

Gian walked back to his desk to prepare an acceptance to move again to Paris. The king's offer still stood—permanent head of Louis XIV's personal Paris Observatory. The world's greatest.

Giovanni Dominic Cassini from Genoa would be a Catholic Frenchman.

—

The old man sat on a dusty mat near the corner of the Paris park. Along this path many of the town people came and went daily, attending to their business.

It was two corners only from the *Academy of Sciences* meeting rooms at the king's Library upriver on the "left" of the Seine. And thus Jean-Dominique Cassini, Academy Fellow, passed here not infrequently. It was not two miles walk westwards from his Observatory.

Cassini adjusted his new wig, learning how it handled a stroll in the breeze.

"Beggars are always a confrontation," complained his companion. "They know it makes us guilty, but the begging is still wrong."

Cassini and his colleague went to pass around.

"You!" called the old man. He jabbed a stick in Cassini's direction.

That fellow's long tangled hair, was it ever washed? Two teeth were missing as he grinned. Cassini did not recall seeing him before.

"You! There's a message for you."

Cassini stopped and turned abruptly. "Message?"

He should continue walking.

"I have been given news for you. You in the big hair."

"You are mistaken, I think," and he made to go.

"Wait. It's from your planet. Or the Dutchman's." He cackled. "It's the truth. It's the last truth."

"What's the truth?"

"Let's go," pleaded his colleague. The Dutchman.

"They are waiting for you in the cold tarry mud, in the ice. They need you. Monsieur, the gods are calling your name. They wait a very long time. You can't escape them by coming here."

"I don't know what you are saying," said Cassini. This beggar couldn't know his name, couldn't know Huygens either.

"He's a dreamer. Just leave him." Christiaan shuffled on, looking back, signalling.

"Monsieur, it's your planets. They have the truth. You want the truth?"

Jean-Dominique Cassini caught up to his friend.

From behind was an extended evil laugh.

—

*Paris 1672.*

*My dear Mr Wren,*

*Christopher,*

*My fondest greetings from Paris. Our world connects as never it has before, hence I am sure you may already know some of the recent events for me across Europe. But is not a letter always the dearest thing to receive?*

*When we met briefly that once fourteen years ago in riot-ravaged London, we could little foresee how much change and knowledge would follow in a short time. For myself, I confess I misjudged how quickly proper governing could be restored in England, and how early your new king granted charter to your prestigious Royal Society. Undoubtedly, its role in enlightening our world has a high value.*

*I am immensely proud to hereby accept the role of Royal Society Fellow which your letter just now arrived has offered to me. But no, no, this letter now is personal. This is not the correct place. I will without delay return to you a further letter with my more formal acceptance.*

*Along with my current position of Director of the King Louis XIV's Paris Observatory, I also consult as Fellow of the Academie des Sciences. I am seriously proud to be contributing, as you do with extravagance, to the academy functions. It is the modern incarnation of our older informal and much-loved Republic of Letters. Our dear colleague Meneer Christiaan Huygens resides here also, also Fellow of the Academie.*

*I know you were in Paris a handful of years ago, studying the magnificent new Baroque constructions of our King Louis. This was the time of the Palace of Versailles, changes to the Louvre, the domes of Val-de-Grace and the Sorbonne. They are all places I love visiting now.*

*Your plans now for St Paul's Cathedral I have seen for myself. They are magnificent. They remind me much of Paris, and I congratulate you.*

*For me, my past few years have given me deep, crippling sadness. I lost my dear wife.*

Jean-Dominique put down his quill.

"Keep looking," was her only final message. "I have loved you, Gian. Thank you."

Then he had nothing. He could not give his farewells. He would not hold her hand, cry with her in her last sorrows. Never could he rage on her coffin. He knew it should have been different. Oh, Celia, my Love.

*During that deepest of grieving, I lost also my beloved assistants of many years, who again were family to me. This spans the time you toured Paris. Had my life been happier then, I would have loved meeting with you in Paris. Paris had pleasant earlier memories for me.*

*Three years ago, King Louis seconded me from Bologna to oversee construction of his Observatory, and you know that, but then he enticed me to come permanently to Paris to direct the Observatory.*

*I have embraced my new country. Like Italy, France is*

　　　　　　　　　　Cassini's Vision

*Catholic, but I am somewhat more at liberty here to release my scientific findings. Perhaps even to speak of my conclusions arising. On that I ought to say not much more, but I am sure you will know my meaning.*

*I still am learning the language and customs, and I do blunder so. But a Frenchman I shall stay.*

*My three children are with me here, in the care of their familiar Italian governess, and all four are quickly becoming Parisians, with some tutoring from a delightful local lass.*

*A funny thing is happening here in the past year. Our Louis the Sun King seems to have decided he no longer likes Paris and his Parisians, and he has retired to his opulent Palace in Versailles. He governs from there. Here we are the world's greatest city (Christopher, let's start a fun argument), we are the largest city, adorned with Louis' superb monuments. And now he is absent. The construction and the big science continues so far. Wide boulevards are replacing the old city walls. But we wonder. ("We". You see, I am a Parisian.)*

Cutting all ties?

Gian, what's out there? Beyond whatever we imagined we might ever know?

You promised me!

*My dear Christopher, in just this one year in Paris, I have made two wildly exciting astronomical findings. To date, I have told few, but my results are nearly ready for publishing as I write to you.*

*My venerable elder Galileo (I told you this long ago: I considered him my mentor) found the moons of planet Jupiter. Our esteemed colleague Huygens first saw the moon we now call Titan near Saturn. I now lay claim to be in the company of these pioneers, albeit a little late. I found two new moons of Saturn I am publishing on. These are the things that make a glow in the heart of a scientist.*

*(And I am starting work now on the rings we see around Saturn. I suspect they are not solid, but rather countless fine fragments. But that's future.)*

*The second finding I am about to publish is this. Using shipboard chronometers and synchronised sightings of scheduled eclipses of Jupiter's moons, I now have a figure for the distance of Mars from the Earth. We knew a while ago the ratios of distances of the Earth, Sun and planets, but we have never had proof before of the real size of those distances.*

*It has been public news that sailing expeditions were underway to make these coordinated observations. But now we have the result. We at long last know the size of our universe. This measurement makes me prouder than the new moons do. This is grand new knowledge.*

*You must wait. I have nearly finished the reports.*

*I have one sorrow. I said above, I will soon publish. But, alas, it is Louis' Academie that will publish my first discovery, my new moons. I am not sure if I will be credited. Be my friend. Remember I told you early.*

*Christopher, thank you for the honour. I know the fellowship award has you behind it.*

*Until we meet again (and we must)*

*Yours*

*Jean-Dominique Cassini*

—

Genevieve was pregnant.

Jean-Dominique's French naturalisation was processed last year, and he had now formed a marriage alliance with a noble family of remarkable wealth. Of the many influential witness signatures on the marriage contract, the most prized was that of Louis XIV himself. The social ranking of Jean-Dominique Cassini of Paris Observatory was created at the highest end of the French nobility.

Genevieve de Laistre came from the Court of Clermont, and her dowry included the opulent Chateau de Thury in the Oise, an excellent choice for a family summer residence. In Paris, Cassini and de Laistre were entitled to free accommodation on the first floor of the Observatory. However, they found that rather cold and draughty, and they were still seeking additional independent space within short distance of the Observatory.

Cassini's three growing children and their Italian governess, and the kitten that had no name as yet, were absorbed quietly into the new noble household. He had sold his Italian identity, but he would not sell away his children, who now used Celia's Bellini name.

In his new social circles, some frowned. A few, in private, expressed their admiration for his stand.

Quality Bellini Italian artworks were hung in the big rooms of the residence. In his study, a small triptych, enigmatic, a scene of a gully near his native Genoa, was hanging on the left wall.

But his dynasty would be built with Genevieve.

—

The "Italian Room" in their Observatory quarters—and Genevieve was generous and tolerant—was dominated by Cassini's Curiosity Cabinet. She would ask him sometimes about the curios that were her man's other story.

Pained? Maybe. Triumphant? Smug? Maybe again. But tolerant more than those. There was a future to make.

So. The miniature ptolemaic planet model, the terracotta cat whose origin no-one could identify, the Italian translation of Abu al-Hasan's *Optics*, that Cassini had paid for so dearly, two old, crude and now naked lens sets, an Islamic scroll of poetry, the intensely coloured perfect sphere of glass, and a Chinese candle, graduated in hours of burning.

Maybe the tryptich of secrets should go to the Italian Room.

—

Christiaan the Dutchman took a carriage to the Observatory occasionally. Sometimes it was a social visit without an agenda, and now and then of a night-time they would check together some stars on Cassini's Campani telescope. Huygens still built his own instruments, but Cassini stuck with the quality Roman designs he had known and trusted since Panzano.

"Hey Jean," Huygens said, "one of my students, and I believe you have had him in class too, keeps questioning me about some old reports of yours."

"He should ask me."

"He says he has asked, but you have not wanted to listen."

"Well, tell me, what report? What student?"

"His name is Ole. Ole Romer."

"Oh, yes, Ole. He is fascinated with the seasonal change in the Jupiter moon eclipses."

"He asks me to explain it, but I knock him back too. It's your area of knowledge, and I don't want to intrude," said Christiaan.

"Intrude? Years ago I reported the observations, noted the variations without further comment, and left the theory to be solved by others smarter than I."

"Jean, Ole keeps trying to put an explanation to you."

                                    Cassini's Vision

"I know. It's not an explanation. He suspects light may have a finite speed through the ether. But that's impossible. Light is instantaneous."

"I've listened to Ole. His theory deserves more consideration. But I've refused to encourage him. As I said, it's your domain."

"Christiaan, you go talk with Ole. You have my permission, if you ever needed it, to tell him to investigate and to make a student report as he sees fit. Let him burn his career."

Huygens looked at Cassini, and stayed silent a few moments.

On Cassini's wall, a Huygens pendulum clock, serial number '5', still lazily counted the ticks dealt out by Celia's godlet.

"I guess it's not the first time we have disagreed on what's out there, is it?"

"Light occurs instantly. It has no property called speed," insisted Cassini.

"Like life could never be out there?"

"Christiaan, my friend," said Jean-Dominique, very slowly, "I know well how to observe facts, exciting, new and verifiable facts, and to record them. I have no intention of speculating or theorising beyond those facts on what any further truth is. I'm choosing to make that not my skill."

# Barcelona 2010

*"Just five years ago, the Huygens probe, built by this Agency, separated from NASA's Cassini spacecraft and landed on Titan, Saturn's moon of deep cold lakes of hydrocarbon. This is for now the only landing of a man-made probe in the outer Solar System. Scientists will gather this month at the CosmoCaixa science museum in Barcelona, to consider future Titan and ice-ring exploration missions."*

*Press release: 8 January 2010, European Space Agency.*

—

Planning is underway for the next space missions to the large planets. The Barcelona gathering is full of spies, multiple agendas, and clandestine side meetings. From the earlier Voyager probe had come the suppressed report on suspicions of activity on the Saturn moons. That was the secret military study, coded *Celia B.*

*Celia B* is now upgraded by the current Cassini-Huygens mission observations, particularly the landing probe data by Huygens, and the continuing visuals from Cassini. It now notes "highly significant signs of responsive life".

No official mission report mentions any of this. What might be actually out there is too dangerous.

# Luna Saturni

*Date: planetary season 163,780,224 since the First Recording.*

—

The slow age-old memories of she who still precariously inhabits the new icy rings around the huge planet, sixth body from the far fiery one. She whose ancient ice moon home is torn up now, the crystal shards inexorably being sucked to the hungry planet.

She. The Lady of the Rings.

She who wonders how the black tarry lakes of the big moon have served those other slow creatures who used to be over there. Have they survived all these aeons? She calls them at intervals, and listens. They have not broadcast anything back since ever their clouds shrouded them from sight.

But someone did pass by. Someone else. She heard them chattering, and then they left. Who were they?

Are They returning, the Great Ones from beyond the stars? Is this our final reckoning? Will we have all failed?

# The Author

Brian Lavery was born in Sydney, a few hours before that first atomic bomb. That's what he blames, anyway.

He's been a monk, a teacher, a hippie, a nomad, a rebel, a corporate geek, a trainer, a world traveller, and now an idler.

He tried surviving Melbourne, Canberra and Darwin, but he settled in Queensland with Robyn, and he wonders where the years went.

Also by Brian Lavery:
*Cassini's Vision*

Published by Brian Lavery:
*White Dawn*
by John J Lee

# Contact Us

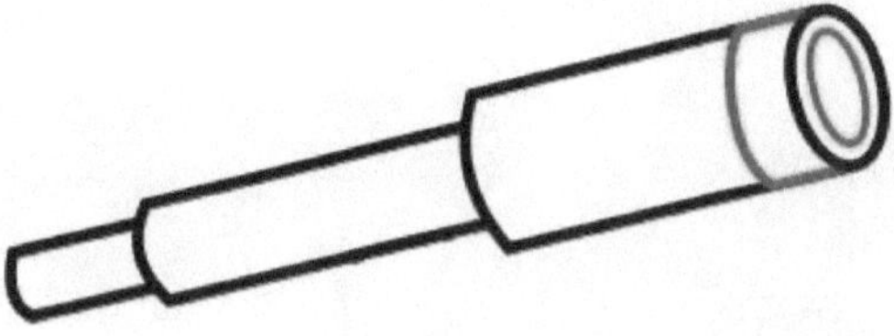

Visit the web page of this book:
**https://cassinisvision.blavery.com**

Or email us at:
**cassinisvision@blavery.com**